VAMPIRELLA®

The Blood Dragon

Dan Wickline

Dynamite Books

VAMPIRELLA: THE BLOOD DRAGON
ISBN: 978-1-5241-1960-7 (print)
978-1-5241-1961-4 (e-book)

Published by: Dynamite Books
A division of Dynamite Entertainment
113 Gaither Dr., Ste. 205 Mt. Laurel, NJ 08054

DYNAMITE®

www.dynamite.com

Nick Barrucci - CEO, Publisher
Juan Collado - President, COO
Brandon Dante Primavera – Vice President of IT & Operations
Joseph Rybrandt – Executive Editor
Matt Idelson – Senior Editor
Kevin Ketner – Editor
Cathleen Heard – Art Director
Alexis Perrson – Graphic Designer
Katie Hildalgo – Graphic Designer
Rachel Kilbury – Digital Multimedia Associate
Jay Spence – Dir of Product Development
Mariano Nicieza – Dir of Research & Development
Jeff Schomber – Production Manager
Amy Jackson – Administrative Coordinator
Alan Payne – Vice President of Sales & Marketing
Vince Faust – Marketing Coordinator
Pat O'Connell – Sales Manager

Dan Wickline – Writers & Book Design
Jordi Penalva - Cover Art
Matt Idleson – Editor
Salome Jones – Copy Editor

First printing 2020.
Printed in the USA

Publisher's Cataloging-in-Publication Data

Names: Wickline, Dan, author.
Title: Vampirella : the blood dragon / Dan Wickline.
Series: Vampirella
Description: Mt. Laurel, NJ: Dynamite Books, 2020.
Identifiers: ISBN: 978-1-5241-1960-7 (pbk.) | 978-1-5241-1961-4 (e-book)
Subjects: LCSH Vampires--Fiction. | Dragons--Fiction. | Cults--Fiction. | Horror. | Fantasy fiction. | Science fiction. | BISAC FICTION / Horror | FICTION / Science Fiction
Classification: LCC PS3623 .I28 V36 2020 | DDC 813.6--dc23

To Steve Niles, for opening the door
to the horror world for this once novice writer.

PROLOGUE

Hua ducked down as low as she could, her knees pressing the pleated front of her long skirt against the cold, muddy ground. She could feel the dampness against her skin, but she wasn't going to move. She wasn't very tall yet, so the rows of wheat were high enough to keep her hidden if she stayed in a crouch. Another month and the stalks would be taller than she was and ready to harvest. That was why she was out here, or rather that was why her brother Fan and her father were out here, talking with a couple of men about working with them to bring in the harvest. Hua was supposed to be helping her mother, but she had hurried through feeding the chickens and quietly followed after when Fan and her father left the house.

This time she had to avoid being seen. Fan had caught her following him last week and made her carry the water back from the well. And before that he made her catch the goat that had gotten out. In truth, Fan had discovered her every time she'd followed him. This time was going to be different. Hua peered through the gaps in the wheat to where they stood.

"We have been very fortunate this year," her father was saying. "The weather has been good, and we were able to lay more seed this time. We'll need a few more men in a month."

One of the visitors rubbed the back of his neck as he spoke. "I will do what I can for you, but you've heard that the Emperor is conscripting able-bodied men to service. I may not have that many extra workers this time."

Her father placed a hand on the man's shoulder. "Whatever help you can provide will be appreciated. My boy and I shall do the rest."

The visitor smiled. "We will see you soon."

The men turned toward the road while her father started back to the house. "Are you coming, Fan?"

Her brother stayed where he was. "I'll be up in a moment, Father. I just want to check something first."

Fan took a few steps into the rows of wheat and gazed out over the golden sea that would provide well for their family. The land had been their grandfather's before he passed it down and one day it would be Fan's to pass on to his son. Hua knew how seriously her brother took that responsibility. In the spring, he would marry Ling, a daughter from a neighboring farm, and her dowry would add more acres to their own land. After the wedding, her father would start building a dowry for Hua so she could find a husband. Hua hoped that would take some time as she was far from done being a child. She didn't see what the rush for Fan to marry was. He was only seventeen.

She'd gotten lost in her thoughts for a moment and before she realized that Fan was walking towards her hiding spot. "Come out, Little Squirrel."

Hua hunched down a little more, certain that her brother was just guessing and had not actually seen her in the field. But the slosh of his feet against the mud told her he was drawing closer. His hand on her shoulder made it impossible to deny. He had caught her again.

She stood, disappointment washing over her. "How did you know?"

"You walk like a horse on gravel." He shook his head. "I heard you following us from the house. Now come with me."

Hua followed after her brother with her head hung low. "What is it I have to do?"

"Hush and keep up." Fan led her through the wheat field towards the edge of their property.

The sound of rushing water grew as they walked. A small river ran along the east side of their farm. It was six to eight feet wide, depending on the amount of rain they'd had, and no more than two feet deep. As they approached it, Hua noticed that the water was running a little faster than normal. A storm had come through the day before, which accounted for the muddy ground as well as the more aggressive current.

Fan stopped on the bank and gestured towards the water. "In you go."

Hua was confused. "Why?"

He pointed down to her dirt-covered skirt. "If mother sees that mud on your clothes, I will be an only child. Now get in there and hopefully everything will dry before you are called in for lunch."

Hua took a step into the cold water and a chill raced through her body. "Maybe I should take it off and..."

"You're wasting time. Just step in, clean the dirt off and get out." Fan put a hand on her back and pushed gently. "Just don't go in too far. I don't want to see you swept out into the ocean."

She moved a little further into the river until the water was halfway up her legs. She reached down and rubbed her hands against the hem of her skirt, trying to knock off as much of the dirt as she could. She hoped the water would warm up once she was in it for a minute, but instead her teeth began to chatter and the muscles in her shoulders ached with cold. She felt like she had gotten enough off and turned to step out when she noticed a pink lotus flower a few feet away. She waded deeper into the river, stretching her arm out to grab the flower. Her foot hit something slippery. She lost her balance and fell backwards, her head dipping under the water before she could catch her breath. The cold water shot into her mouth and nose as she reached out for anything to pull herself back up.

She flailed around until she got her face out of the water for a moment and she could suck in a breath. She saw her brother break into a run to get ahead of her as the current began to carry her away. She kicked, trying to keep her face above the water, but her skirt wrapped around her legs, pulling her under. Her lungs were burning and she longed to take another breath. She knew she should not pull water into her lungs, but the urge to breathe was so strong. Just as she was about to give in, she felt a tug at her shirt. It was Fan! She felt his hand open and close, getting a better grip and then he pulled her up and into his arms. Hua coughed as she drew in air and tried to get the water out of her throat. Her brother carried her carefully back onto solid ground.

"It's all right, Little Squirrel, I've got you." He held her until she was breathing normally again and had stopped shaking.

He placed her down gently and squatted down to check her skirt. Seeing that the water had done its job, he took her by the hand and silently led her back through the wheat field towards their house. The sun was out, but it wouldn't be warm enough to dry her clothes or hair on the walk back.

Their mother was outside when they got there. She took in Hua's condition. "What have you been up to, Hua?"

The girl couldn't bring herself to speak. She knew she would be in trouble for following her brother and father. She desperately tried to think of something to say as Fan began to speak.

"She asked me to go with her to the river." He squeezed her hand gently. "She had seen a flower by the bank she wanted to get for you. But the ground was slippery from the rain and she fell in. I was able to pull her out quickly, but as you can see her clothes will need some time to dry."

Her mother appeared skeptical, looking at her to see if the story was true. Hua stood as still as she could, trying to fight off the chill of the wet clothes. Fan reached into his shirt and pulled out a pink lotus flower on a long green stem. He handed it to Hua, who took it reluctantly. He then pushed her forward so she could give it to her mother. Her mother's skeptical gaze melted into a big smile. She took the flower and gave Hua a kiss on the forehead.

"It is a wonderful gift. And I am glad you were wise and asked your brother to go with you." She took Hua by the hand. "Come now, let's get you some dry clothes."

Hua followed after her mother but glanced back to see Fan. He smiled and nodded at her, then he turned and went back out to finish his chores for the day. Hua found herself smiling too.

The wheat continued to grow until it reached high enough that Hua could stand up straight and not be seen. Fan and her father had led the workers into the fields for three days straight and were preparing for a fourth with a hearty breakfast. The sound of the workers' horses seemed to be earlier on this morning, but not so much as to alarm Hua. The look on her father's face did though.

He got up and went to the window. "They are riding too fast."

"Perhaps they are eager to finish here and move on to another farm," Fan offered, continuing to eat. "We should get a good day's work out of them."

Her father still seemed concerned. "There are too many horses coming. Something is wrong."

Hua listened more carefully. It did seem like more hooves clattering down the road than in the days before. A lot more. She glanced at her brother, worry starting to build inside of her. He rested his hand on hers and gave her a reassuring smile before he patted her hand and got up to follow their father outside to meet the riders. Hua gave them a moment, then dashed out after them. She stayed back a few feet but followed them out along the dirt path to the road. As the riders approached, the noise grew louder and louder, until it could only be described as thunderous. When they got far enough out past the wheat, she could finally see a half dozen riders quickly approaching. Her father had been right. They weren't farm hands at all, rather a troop of soldiers riding in pairs. They came to a halt just shy of where Fan and her father stood.

One of the soldiers appeared a little more decorated than the others. He pulled a scroll from inside his tunic and read it out. "By edict of Zhengde Emperor, all able-bodied males are being conscripted into service immediately. You are to be prepared to leave by dawn two days hence."

Fan looked shocked and tried to speak, but his father stepped in front of him. "I beseech you, humbly. We are but farmers and as you can see, our fields need harvesting, or our family will starve. I will be honored to serve the Emperor, but I implore you to let my son stay and finish working the fields in my place."

"I am told you have two children." The soldier looked towards the house. "Where is your other child?"

Hua stepped out of the wheat stalks where she had tried to hide. “I am here.”

Her father turned, not at all surprised to see her. He reached out a hand, gesturing her to come forward. “As you can see, I was blessed with both a son and a daughter. And while she is growing fast, she can’t do a third of what her brother can in the fields.”

“The Emperor is not without compassion.” The soldier tucked the scroll back into place. “He has given instructions for situations like this. You may stay and tend your fields, but your son is to come with us.”

“I should’ve known that the Emperor in his infinite wisdom would’ve foreseen this.” Her father lowered his head in respect. “But my son has never been to battle, while I have served the Emperor once before. Surely my experience would make me a better choice to come with you.”

“The Emperor’s orders are clear. Your son is to be ready with a mount at dawn in two days. We will be riding hard to Guangzhou to join the rest of the forces.” He nodded to the other soldiers and they turned and began to ride off. “Do not make us come looking for him or we will take you both.”

As the soldiers cantered away, Hua raced over and wrapped her arms around her brother’s waist, tears pouring from her eyes. “You can’t go! Please, Father, don’t let them take Fan!”

Her father knelt down beside her. “I don’t want him to go either, but we can’t disobey the Emperor.”

“It will be okay.” Fan tucked a lock of hair behind her ear. “I will be back before you know it.”

He took her by the hand and led her back to the house so they could tell their mother of the news and prepare for the workday. Hua went along, but the tears continued to flow.

The day Fan was to leave came quickly. As the sun rose, Hua and her family stood by the side of the road. Hua held Fan's hand as their mother hugged him and their father checked the saddle on the horse for the fourth time. Their parents said their goodbyes and returned to the house.

"Why are you going?" Hua asked.

"Because the Emperor commanded it," Fan said simply. "I must go."

"You could head north, away from the fighting. Hide for a while until the war ends and then come home," Hua pleaded. "Please, Fan. Don't go with the soldiers. Run and be safe."

"But I wouldn't be safe. I would bring shame upon our family." He continued to watch the road. "They would take Father with them and then there would be no one here to harvest the fields. No one to take what has been harvested to the market. You and Mama would have no money or food. All of that just so I did not go to war. How could I live with myself if I did that?"

She tried to wipe away her tears. "What if you die in the war?"

"Then I will have died with honor." He looked down at her. "And you will tell them to bury my body down by the river. Plant a lotus flower near my grave. When it blooms you will know that I am looking down over you and that I will always be with you."

She squeezed his hand tightly as fresh tears began to fall. She didn't want to think of him dying, but she vowed to do exactly what he asked if that happened. Hua stayed next to her brother until they heard approaching hooves. The sound made her heart sink. It was time.

Fan leaned down and gave his sister a hug. "Be good, Little Squirrel. Take care of our parents until I return."

"I will." Her voice cracked as the tears rolled down her cheeks. "Don't be gone long. I will miss you."

He kissed her on the forehead, then took the reins of the horse in hand. He effortlessly swung up onto the brown mare before smiling back down at her. The thunderous noise grew far louder than before as Hua watched over twenty riders pass by. Four of the original soldiers were in the lead followed by a motley group of farmers and merchants that they had pulled together. Fan kicked his horse forward and joined in at the tail end of the group that was trailed by the final two soldiers. Hua stepped out into the road and watched until they had vanished in the distance.

CHAPTER ONE

The sun was just starting to rise over the city of Van Nuys as five black clad figures walked across the tarmac to the awaiting Gulfstream G650. The engine was already revving, and the co-pilot stood at the bottom of the steps to meet the passengers. The three men and two women of various nationalities carried only a single bag each. One of the man nodded to the co-pilot and then headed up the stairs, the others following quickly. Once inside they stowed their bags and took seats as the co-pilot retracted the stairs and secured the door.

"Good morning, everyone. I'm Frank," the co-pilot announced. "Your pilot is Captain Robbins, and she'll be getting us in the air in just a few moments. The flight time to Hong Kong looks to be just shy of sixteen hours, which will have us arriving just after ten pm local time. Once we reach our cruising altitude, you're welcome to use your electronic devices and we are wifi enabled. If you need anything during the flight, Ella will be here to assist you."

At the mention of her name, Ella stepped into the walkway where everyone could see her. She wore a powder blue skirt and blouse accented with dark blue trim and a matching dark blue scarf. Her long, jet black hair was curled up into a bun and held in place by a decorative set of chop sticks. She made eye contact with each of the passengers before nodding and moving back to the rear of the cabin.

Frank spoke to get everyone's attention back. "There are safety instruction cards on the tables in front of you. Please take a moment to read them as we prepare for takeoff. Thank you for choosing Goodwin Charters and have a nice flight."

The passengers settled in and buckled their belts as the plane began to taxi out to the runway. Ella's seat was back in the galley area where the premade meals and beverages were kept. From that vantage she could see them all. Nearest to her on the right-hand side of the plane was a tall, thin woman with dark skin, her hair pulled back into a clip. In front of her was a short, stocky Asian man with a shaved head and a pencil-thin mustache. On the left-side was a muscular, tanned man with brown wavy hair and a close-trimmed goatee. A curvy, blond woman sat facing him and in the seat closest to the cockpit was an angular Hispanic man with slicked-back black hair. They sat silently, looking at anything but each other as the plane gained speed and lifted off the ground.

After a few moments, the seatbelt sign went out and Ella got to her feet. She wheeled the drink cart out from its slot and stopped at the first passenger. "Would you care for a drink?"

"I'll have a beer," the woman responded in what sounded like Portuguese accented English.

The Asian man just shook his head while the man on her left with the Texas drawl asked for a bourbon, neat. Ella heard a Montreal accent from the blonde who asked for a white wine. The last man was definitely from New York, but Ella couldn't pin down which borough from the few words he said as he took two small bottles of tequila and asked for a lime and salt. As she rolled the cart back, the passengers began looking at their phones or checking their laptops and one started reading a book. No one conversed. If anything, they all purposely ignored each other .

As the long flight continued, Ella made sure that everyone's drinks were full, served breakfast and lunch at the appropriate times and took the opportunities that presented themselves. The Texan got up to use the lavatory, and she caught him as he exited, asking him to help her pull out a jammed tray. He had no problem at all getting it unstuck.

"Thank you." She smiled. "The lovely lady next to you, is that your wife?"

He seemed surprised by the question. "No. I've never met her before. Why do you ask?"

"I've just noticed the way she keeps looking over at you." Ella started putting away trays. "She seemed to have a lot of affection in her eyes. But I must be reading it wrong. Thank you again for your help."

The man glanced over at the blonde before shaking his head and returning to his seat. When he sat down, he was turned a little more towards the woman and smiled at her. She smiled back. Ella watched the whole thing and then focused on the other passengers. A little while later when the woman with the Portuguese accent got up to stretch, Ella gestured her back to the galley.

"Are you all right, ma'am?" Ella gave her a serious look.

The woman seemed confused. "Yes. Why wouldn't I be?"

"I've been a flight attendant for a long time, and I can tell when there is tension between two passengers." She leaned in closer. "I've been watching how the gentleman at the front of the plane keeps glaring back at you. If you need help, tell me and I can notify the pilot and have authorities waiting when we land."

"I'm afraid you have read this all wrong. I don't even know that man and haven't seen him looking at me."

Ella gave her a friendly smile. "I'm glad I'm wrong then. You're from Brazil, aren't you?

The woman nodded. "How did you...?"

"Your accent. And at least you have your friend sitting with you."

"He's not my..." The woman glanced over her shoulder back to the cabin just as the Hispanic man looked back at her. "Never mind. Everything is fine."

Ella watched as the woman returned to her seat. It was only a few minutes before the man at the front looked back at all the passengers again, something he'd been doing every few minutes the entire flight. Ella walked back up the aisle to check on everyone's drinks. The two on the left had already started talking and the woman was explaining how recruiting was going up in Canada. The Brazilian woman was now asking the Asian man about the guy at the front, if he knew him. She checked if any of them needed anything but ignored the Hispanic man, walking past and knocking on the cockpit door. When she heard the click of it unlocking, she went in and, keeping her voice low, asked if they needed anything. They were fine at that moment. She returned to the passenger cabin, made certain the door was closed behind her and turned to walk back. She looked towards the man in the front seat. When he made eye contact, she nervously looked away and hurried down the aisle.

Now people were talking, and Ella was listening. When you have a bunch of strangers starting to talk, they go to the subject they have in common, and in this case, it was the crazy-ass cult they were in. She picked up some names. Dave and Jocelyn talked about how they got involved with the group. James and Maria exchanged rumors about the guy in the front named Carlos, they believed, who recruited some of the most unworthy members.

And Carlos kept staring at the cockpit door or back at the galley, which made the others nervous.

After serving dinner and a few more drinks, the conversations were flowing even better. Jocelyn seemed open to the idea of getting drinks after they arrived. "You never know, with the world going to be changing and all. I'm up for some fun."

"I know of a club about a block away from where we're supposed to meet." Dave had his southern charm going. "It's a new place called Ozone over at the Ritz-Carlton."

"Have you been to Hong Kong before?"

"No. Once I got the address," he tapped his pocket, "I looked the area up to see what was around."

Jocelyn gave him an approving look. "I like a man who prepares."

Ella did too. Knowing the general area where they were going would make following a lot easier. And she knew of Ozone as it was famous for being the highest bar and pool in the world, being on the 118th floor of the International Commerce Centre. They would be landing soon, but she continued to listen to the two conversations, hoping to pick up anything more on the big event coming up. The next thing she heard, though, was the ping of Carlos getting a text message. He checked his phone, sent a message back and quickly got a reply. He then tucked his phone away and got to his feet. From behind his back he pulled out a pair of ornate, doubled-edged daggers and turned towards the back of the plane.

James got to his feet immediately. "What the hell, man?"

"One of our people back in L.A. sent me a message." He took a few steps down the aisle. "Ground crew found an unconscious woman in the staff parking lot. Only thing stolen was her Goodwin Charter flight attendant uniform."

Everyone turned to look at Ella as she reached up and pulled the chop sticks from her hair, letting it fall down to its full length, halfway down her back. "I knew this was going too well."

Dave pulled a Bowie knife from his boot and then got to his feet. Maria slammed out an extendable baton and stood next to James. Jocelyn was the last to rise, reaching into her coat pocket for a pair of brass knuckles. She then removed her coat, laid it on the seat and slipped the knuckles onto her right hand.

Ella looked around at the imposing group. "Airport security is really lacking these days."

Maria pointed at her with the baton. "One chance. Who do you work for?"

"I'm more of a hobbyist." Ella sized up her situation. "I like to stop religious zealots from trying to destroy the world in my free time."

"Just kill her!" Carlos shouted.

Dave and Maria were the closest and moved together. She swung the baton at Ella's knee while Dave swung the knife at her neck. Ella shifted her weight, causing the baton to just glance off her thigh, and pulled back enough that the blade cut across her scarf but missed cutting into her altogether. She caught Dave's elbow with her left hand, forcing his arm to stay exposed and then driving the chopsticks into his wrist with her free hand. The sticks buried in about two inches as blood sprayed out across the cabin. He dropped the Bowie knife, which Ella caught before it could hit the floor. She flung it down the aisle towards Carlos. The large blade wasn't meant for throwing and drifted off course slightly, cutting the man across the arm before sailing past and slamming into the cockpit door.

James lashed out with a kick into Ella's midsection that sent her staggering back a step. Maria took another swing with the baton, this time aiming for Ella's head. With a quick palm-strike, Ella redirected the attack and the baton struck Dave in the temple while he was focused on pulling the sticks out of his wrist. He collapsed like a marionette with its strings cut.

Ella saw a flash out of the corner of her eye and was just able to shift as Jocelyn's brass knuckles narrowly missed her jaw and crashed hard into her shoulder. Then James sent a heel-thrust to her right knee knocking her off balance as Maria moved in for another strike. Ella let her momentum carry her, flipping onto her back and brought the toe of her boot up into Maria's throat. The woman dropped her baton and reached for her crushed windpipe. As she gasped for air, James pushed her aside and tried to stomp down on the prone Ella. The faux flight attendant shifted onto her side, out of the way of the strike. She then punched straight up into the man's exposed groin so hard he instantly doubled over. Ella pulled roughly on his shirt, forcing him into Jocelyn and then knocking them both to the floor.

Carlos was finally clear to move forward just as Ella flipped back onto her feet, coming up with the baton in her hand. He moved in and slashed with the dagger in his right hand, which Ella dodged, then he jabbed with the left, which she was just able to knock away with the baton. He was extremely aggressive and fast, one strike after another. If his opponent had been anyone else, she'd be dead already. But she didn't stay on the defensive long, backing up until he was in the closer quarters of the galley. He couldn't get as much energy behind his swings and he was forced to attack straight forward. He thrust out with both blades towards her stomach, but she dropped the baton and grabbed his wrists. His face took on a surprised expression as he couldn't pull away. She yanked hard on his arms, forcing him down and towards her as she ran her knee up into his chest. The crack of ribs breaking filled the tight space and he gasped in pain. She released his wrists, and the cultist stood up straight, trying to get air in his lungs. She put everything she had into a punch, centered on his chest, the blow knocked him off his feet and sent the man flying down the length of the aisle, where he landed in front of the cockpit door.

Just then the co-pilot poked his head out. "What the hell is going on our here?"

"Go back inside!" Ella yelled.

Frank took a quick look around the cabin. His face went pale, and he slammed the door shut. Carlos and Dave were both out cold. Maria was squirming on the floor, clutching at her destroyed throat. James and Jocelyn were back on their feet. Jocelyn seemed unsure of what to do while James was angry and charged at Ella. She stood her ground and allowed herself to be tackled, leaving James open to a head butt to the bridge of his nose. The snapping sound and rush of blood didn't slow him down as he rammed her into the lavatory door. Ella slammed her forehead down again, focusing on the eyebrow ridge. It took a third strike before his grip loosened. He staggered back just enough that Ella could bring up a palm strike to his face, driving the broken nose bone up into his frontal lobe.

As James's body collapsed to the floor, Jocelyn stared at the woman who has made short work of her companions. "Who are you?"

"I told you, someone who stops crazy idiots like you from trying to destroy the world."

Ella reached down and grabbed the front of her blood-stained and torn uniform, ripping it off with ease. Another tug and the skirt tore away revealing a skintight red suit and high white collar. In the blink of an eye, she dashed across the cabin and took Jocelyn by the throat, pinning her against the wall.

Baring her fangs, she leaned in close. "Where is your meeting?"

Fear raced across the Canadian woman's face. "The waterfront... block one.... The exact address is in my pocket."

Vampirella fished around in the woman's pocket and pulled out a post-it note. She glanced at it to make sure the address was there. She gave Jocelyn a thin smile and tossed her across the room, where she slammed off the front wall of the cabin and dropped on top of the unconscious Carlos. Vampirella crossed the cabin to where they lay, scooped up one of Carlos's daggers and tucked it into her boot. Then she moved to the door of the jet and started to open it.

"Wait! You can't do that!" Jocelyn croaked up at her.

"Why not?" Vampirella grinned wickedly. "Can't you fly?"

She forced open the door and leapt out. As she fell, she watched as things were sucked out of the suddenly decompressing cabin, including the five cultists and what was left of her uniform. She spread her body wide out like a skydiver trying to slow their descent. She could feel it as the two sharp points began to protrude from her back, one from each shoulder blade. The bone-like objects grew quickly and extended so she could see them on either side of her, forming into a pair of smooth, black bat-like wings more than twice her height from tip to tip. With the wings fully extended, the wind caught under them and gave her a rush of exaltation as she swooped up. She took a good look at what was in front of her. Laid out on the horizon were the city lights of Hong Kong.

CHAPTER TWO

As Vampirella's mighty wings carried her down to just above the rooftops of the tallest buildings in Hong Kong, she listened for certain sounds. She didn't know the city. She had visited once, many years before, but now knew of only one contact that might be useful. She needed to be able to move about the city without drawing too much attention to herself. Soaring between a pair of skyscrapers, her heightened hearing picked up a low, repetitive thumping in the distance. With a single, powerful thrust of her wings, she propelled herself towards the noise.

She banked in and circled around the source of the thumping, a three-story building in the middle of a car-filled street. The location didn't stand out from the structures around it at all. If anything, it would be missed on a casual glance as boring and unremarkable—a dull gray building with few windows and no exterior markings to show who occupied it. But as she glided down onto the roof, she could feel the reverberation of the sound coming up from below. She crossed the sun-bleached asphalt to the roof access hatch in the far corner. She grasped the lid. It didn't immediately open, but after a quick yank, it flew back, revealing a square entryway. The repetitive thumping grew louder, now joined by a cacophony of techno sounds and people screaming.

Like with every other city, Vampirella felt it was a safe bet that there would be an underground rave or pop-up club going on where a woman in a red sling suit and shiny black boots wouldn't stand out. She paused long enough to retract her wings. The large, bat-like extensions collapsed in on themselves and she felt them disappear into her shoulder blades as if they'd never existed. She swung her foot over and into the square opening, making contact with one of the metal rungs on the awaiting ladder. She climbed down, pulling the hatch shut behind her. At the bottom of the ladder she found herself in a room filled with file cabinets and storage boxes, light coming through a translucent glass panel in the door. As she approached the door, she could hear nothing on the other side but the techno music she could tell was at least one floor below her.

She opened the door into an empty corridor and followed it until she found stairs that took her down to the second floor. She stepped out into another hallway, this time strewn with people in various stages of making out or doing drugs. She strode past them, keeping her eye out for the things she wanted. At the end of the hall she opened another door, this one taking her into the main dance area. Strobe lights swirled along the walls and ceiling while the music drowned out every other sound. She glanced around the room. It was hard to see anything except shapes through the lightning effects and mass of people, but after a few seconds she found what she was looking for. She approached a slender Caucasian man dressed in black from his thin tie and dress shirt to his leather overcoat.

He saw Vampirella approach, turning to smile at her. He put his hands on either side of his mouth and shouted over the music, "I love your outfit."

"Thanks. But it has no pockets," she yelled back. She made eye-contact with him, gazing deep into his soul. "Give me your coat."

Without hesitation, the man stripped off the coat and held it out to her. "Sure thing."

She slid her arms in and pulled the soft leather around her. "I also need some cash."

"Take what you need." He held out his wallet.

She opened it and pulled out the paper currency. There was 2,500 Hong Kong dollars, which she figured to be about 320 American dollars. She left the credit cards and gave him back the wallet. She gestured for him to turn around. He smiled, tucked his wallet away and turned back to face the DJ. She melted into the crowd, easily streaming through the throng of people and making her way towards the exit. Once out on the street, she flagged down a taxi.

The drive looked her over as she got in, then asked in English, "Where to, Miss?"

"Waterfront district. Block one."

"You got it." He flipped on the meter then guided the car away from the curb.

It wasn't a long drive, fifteen minutes tops, but it was enough for her to try and take in the feel of Hong Kong. A major, cosmopolitan city on the surface but steeped in tradition and culture in the side streets and alleyways. An Eastern city that had been dominated by Western culture for too long a time, but when the city reverted to control by China, the country's rich history returned. And while the city seemed to be vibrant and welcoming, it still cast long shadows where evil hid, waiting for its next victim.

The taxi came to a stop. The driver turned to face her. "Want me to wait?"

"No." She paid for the ride and slipped out of the back seat.

Once on the sidewalk, she fished the slip of paper out of her boot and read the address of the cultists' meeting place. The

Grand Waterfront was a series of six, sixty-two story buildings laid out with blocks one, two and three stacked close together, then five and a shopping mall in the middle and six and seven on the far side. There was no block four, at least not that she could see. She wondered why. She walked towards the building she wanted, looking around to spot any cameras. There were a few outside and a couple in the lobby. There was also a reception desk with a guard on duty.

She stood in front of the building, pretending to be waiting for a ride. She was lined up perfectly with the front door and listened closely to the sounds coming from inside. When she heard the bell signaling that an elevator was about to open in the lobby, she took off. She was in the door, across the marble floor, past the exiting passenger and in through the open door before the guard was able to look up from his desk. She knew the cameras would have recorded nothing more than a blur of motion.

A ride up to the 38th floor and Vampirella made her way to the apartment listed on the paper. Just outside the door, she pretended to search for something in the pockets of the leather coat, while listening for movement inside. She had to filter out the noises from the other apartments, focusing just on the space behind the door marked '17.' When she heard nothing, she took a deep breath in through her nose, taking in the smells of the place. There was the scent of food. Noodles and pork, to be specific. She could get down to the types of spices, but that wasn't important. But there was one scent she couldn't place. It was musty, old. almost like decay, but different. The one thing she was certain of was that there was no one inside the apartment.

She tried the handle and was surprised to find it unlocked. A quick turn and she moved inside. The door opened into a small hallway with a closet on the left and an entrance into the kitchen on the right. The hallway continued into what looked to be the main living area. She silently moved into the kitchen, careful of her steps as she walked onto the tiled floor. There were a few dishes in the sink and a pan on the stove with remnants of pork chow fun clinging to the side. A trash can in the corner was half full with more of the chow fun and a few paper plates on the top. An open beer sat on the counter with the cap and bottle opener inches away. Beads of condensation still clung to the green glass.

She moved into the living room where she found a couple of nice couches with the pillows askew or on the floor. On a side table were a few sheets of paper. She crossed the room and took a look. It was a printout of the weather for the area for the next week. The fifth of the month had been highlighted in yellow. The additional pages were a list of things to do in the city for that same time period. She folded the papers and tucked them into her coat pocket. A glance around the living room showed nothing else. No magazines, books or photographs. Nothing you'd expect to see in someone's home.

She continued to search. There was a bedroom off of the kitchen area. It seemed small to her, with only a twin bed, dresser desk and closet. Again, there was nothing personal in it, more like a room waiting for an occupant. There was a bathroom next to it that had signs of use, trash in the bin, towels askew, but no razors, medicine, makeup or toothbrushes. She moved to the other end of the apartment, where she checked the door to the balcony. It was unlocked. There were a couple of chairs outside, positioned to look out over the city. She continued on.

The apartment was surprisingly large, close to two thousand square feet if she had to guess. She started down the other hallways to the first of four bedrooms. The door was already open allowing her to look around the room quickly. It contained two beds against opposite walls. Both appeared to have been slept in. The closet door stood open, but nothing hung inside. She moved on to the next room and found it in a similar condition. One bed made, the other disheveled. Closet empty and no other signs anyone had been there.

The door to the third room was closed and she decided to skip it and look into the open fourth room. This was the master bedroom with its own bathroom. It had three twin beds in it, all made. The closet door was closed, but the closet was empty when she looked inside. The bathroom was untouched. No one had been in this room since the last time it was made up and a fine layer of dust on the blankets told her it had been this way for at least a few days. She headed back to the closed door. She heard nothing from inside, but the musty smell she had picked up earlier was even stronger here. She reached for the handle and turned it slowly. The room inside was similar to the first two with twin beds on opposite sides, both made. The big difference here was the four people standing stone still in the center of the room.

Vampirella took a fighting stance, expecting to be attacked. They didn't move. She waited, tensed to spring but nothing happened. She decided to move in and get a closer look. All four were male, various heights and weights, but all relatively young looking. Early to mid-twenties. They wore similar outfits, possibly some kind of uniforms. They were traditional looking, dark gray pants and coats. The coats had long, billowing sleeves that covered their hands completely, a strip of black running over the left shoulder and a red dragon emblem sitting over the chest. All wore dark gray, circular hats that fit tightly on their heads. Their skin was sickly pale, and each had a series of Chinese letters down the right side of their face from scalp to neck to clavicle. The letters interested her the most and she moved in closer to see if they were written on or tattooed.

As she got in close enough to see that the ink was permanent, her finger gently brushed against the first man's check. His eyes shot open, his arm swung out quickly, catching Vampirella by surprise and knocking her across the room and through the closet door. She hit the ground inside the closet and sprang back up to her feet, knocking the splintered wood aside. As she stepped back into the room, she saw that all four of the men were now awake and looking at her.

The first one charged her inhumanly fast, swinging his arm like a club. She blocked the stiff limb with her forearm and punched at it with her other fist. The blow hit the man in the chest and sent him stumbling back into his friends. She flashed her fangs and leapt across the room towards them. The four men scattered almost as fast a Vampirella moved. She caught herself before tumbling onto one of the beds. She turned to see three of the men racing out of the room while the fourth was charging at her, swinging his arm down towards her again. She sidestepped the blow and drove her heel into the side of his knee. It didn't bend or give, instead the man stumbled back into the dresser. He grabbed the piece of furniture and spun it around so quickly it caught Vampirella by surprise, clipping her across the arm and turning her completely around.

When she turned back, the man was out of the room and moving down the hallway. His movement was fast but odd. Not really running, he hopped along quickly on straight legs. Vampirella dashed after him, grabbing the back of his coat just as he reached for the balcony door. He quickly spun out of her grasp, swinging his arms around like a human top, forcing her to drop down to avoid them. By ducking low, she had a clear shot at his midsection. She punched out with both hands into his stomach with every ounce of strength she had. He flew back into the metal door frame, bounced off and back towards her. He stumbled past her a little and she sprang up, grabbed him by the back of the head and spun him around a second time, this time driving his face through the glass door, shards flying every direction.

Expecting to see blood streaming out of the wounds on his face, she pulled him back. While his skin was cut to ribbons, there wasn't a drop of blood to be seen. The outside air whistled in through the broken window. As she looked closer, she realized the skin was more than cut. It seemed to have torn away in places revealing the skull beneath. The wounds were getting bigger and his skin was starting to flake off. A gust of wind poured through the broken glass, blowing more and more skin off of his body like dust. The skull underneath also began to disintegrate as she watched. It eroded away in the breeze at a faster and faster pace until there was nothing there but the clothes he had been wearing. She dropped them in a pile on the floor and stepped out onto the balcony. There was no sign of the other three men.

She stepped back into the apartment and did a quick tour through the rooms once more. There was nothing else to learn there. She grabbed the coat with the dragon emblem and knocked off any of the residual dust. She'd come looking for answers but now she just had more questions. She was going to need some help.

CHAPTER THREE

When Vampirella heard through her informants that something big was coming, all she knew was that a group of cultists were going to fly to Hong Kong. Her plan was to be onboard, get as much information as she could overhear and then follow them to their final destination. That plan went out the window, or rather the jet door, the moment she got made. Now she knew that the supernatural was definitely involved. She had that and the dragon symbol, which was very little to go on. She needed more information and the only contact she had in the city was a bit questionable. But she had no other options.

The taxi driver knew exactly where Shanghaied was, but he did his best to talk her out of going there. "That's a bad place, lady. How about I take you to one of the hotel bars instead?"

"Take me to Shanghaied," she said simply as she stared into his eyes.

The driver was silent for a second and then nodded. Turning the wheel, he pulled out into the evening traffic without another word. Vampirella leaned back against the seat and looked out the side window. Out of the corner of her eye she caught the flash of something along the roof tops. Something was moving fast and trying to keep up with the taxi. She did her best to keep an eye on it, but after a few turns, whatever had been following them was gone.

The drive to the outer edge of the city didn't take long with how late it was. Twenty minutes later the cab pulled to a stop and let her out. The driver looked like he wanted to protest leaving a woman alone in a rough neighborhood, but when he looked up to speak he found himself reluctant to open his mouth. Instead he waited for the door to close and sped away.

From outside, the bar was fairly nondescript. The window in the front had a golden-sailed junk in rough waters just above the word 'Shanghaied'. A couple of neon beer logo lights shone through the tinted glass but little else could be seen. The building was gray brick with a wooden door and a simple brass knob. The only other way she could tell it was a bar was the line of motorcycles and drunks lining the front of it. Vampirella made sure her coat was closed before heading towards the door. Just before going in, she glanced over her shoulder, checking the rooftops around her. She saw nothing but couldn't shake the feeling she was being watched.

The inside of the bar was very different. She took in the long, skinny room with the bar top running just in front of the left hand wall, about three quarters of the way to the back. A dozen stools lined up in front of it and ended just before the back wall where there was a door into a rear area. Along the right wall was a series of four-person tables and chairs with a couple extra chairs against the back wall. Everything looked old and well cared for. Behind the bar were shelves for the alcohol and a long mirror. The right wall and the back were painted with a series of ornate murals done in black and gold on red backgrounds depicting battles from Chinese mythology. The closest one to the front door depicted the Monkey King going up against a dozen warriors.

The surprising thing about the bar was the fact that there was only one person in it. With all the people outside she expected it to be packed, but the only person in sight was the bartender. He was an older man with graying black hair slicked back and combed up into a pompadour. He wore a well fitted black suit with a white shirt and a skinny black tie with a gold tie clip. When he looked up and saw her, he flashed a perfect white smile and gestured to the stool in front of him.

"Please, come in and have a drink." His English was near flawless with just a hint of a local accent.

She walked to the bar and took the stool next to the one he had pointed at. He smiled again and reached under the bar for a bottle. There was no label on the dusty brown glass. It had a white ceramic top that was held in place by a metal bar. He pulled out a rocks glass, but added no ice. He flipped the stopper with his thumb, then poured. What came out was a thick, red liquid that gave off a coppery smell. She watched him intently as he added a small, black stirring stick topped with a molded, ornamental sailing ship like the one on the window. He slid the glass over to her and re-affixed the stopper to the bottle.

"You obviously know who I am." She took a sip of the drink, the blood rolling down the back of her tongue and immediately erasing any fatigue she had from the day.

"Of course, Miss Vampirella. I was told you might be stopping by." He gave a quick bow. "I am Zhang Wei."

She placed her drink back on the bar. "The son of Ta Shi Sheng, the infamous Dragon Lady. Keeping up the family business?"

"I have no interest in the criminal underworld." He gestured towards the bar. "I am simply a small business owner. Everything you can buy here is perfectly legal."

"I'm sure your mother was very disappointed in your life choices." She casually turned her glass. "I'm told that you have your ear to the ground when it comes to the more bizarre things happening in this city."

"The Chinese culture is filled with stories of amazing creatures, both good and evil. They make for very entertaining stories." He moved closer to her. "But then I heard tales of real magic, vampires and women who can turn into jungle cats. I became fascinated. Trying to figure out what was real and what was just ancient farmers trying to explain where the sun went every night. As you probably know, once you start looking into the shadows, they start looking back."

She slid her hand through her hair, looking up at him with her mouth open just enough to show her fangs. "Sounds like I've come to the right place."

Excitement showed across his face. "How can I be of service to you?"

"Let's start with this." She pulled Carlos' dagger from her boot and placed it on the bar. "I took this off a guy with a very bad attitude."

Zhang picked up the knife and turned it over in his hand a couple times. "Good balance."

"He had a pair of them." She gestured to the handle. "But I'm more interested in the markings."

He held the dagger up and looked at the ornate Chinese dragon on the handle. He ran his finger over it, feeling the raised edges. "Servants of the Blood. I'd guess someone very high up in the chain of command."

"Of the Blood?" She let out a low whistle. "Who are these people?"

"They're a small cult that worships Xuè Lóng." He held up the symbol to her. "He's also known as the Blood Dragon. These guys are supposed to be preparing the world for his return. Usual cultist garbage. There aren't many in the group, but I've heard their reach is global."

"And what is this Blood Dragon?" She took another drink.

"All mythologies have their story of creation." He walked towards the back wall and pointed at one of the murals. "This is one of them. Not a widely-known one."

"The world was once filled with demons." He ran his finger over a regal looking figure on a throne hovering over a series of demonic looking figures. "The Jade Emperor, upon splitting the world into three parts, heaven, hell and Earth, he banished the demons and left the Sun and the Moon to guard mankind."

He moved his hand over to an image of the Earth with the sun and the moon on either side. He took a few steps, until he stood in front of a part of the mural that looked similar to the image on the dagger.

"Xuè Lóng was one of the banished demons," He rested his hand there. "It's said he foresaw what the Jade Emperor was going to do and prepared a way to return. His followers believe that he still influences mankind in the moments when the guards are not watching."

"And how does this tie into it?" She reached into her coat and pulled out the jacket from the apartment and placed it on the bar. "I found this on one of four extremely pale men with tattooed writing on their faces and what appeared to be an inability to bend their knees and elbows. They had far more strength and speed than a normal person. And after I put the owner of this coat through a glass door, he crumbled into dust. Does that ring any bells?"

Zhang's eyes grew wide. "Jiangshi."

Vampirella turned on her bar stool, following the man as he moved. "Who is Jiangshi?"

"Not a who. A what." He crossed the room to the far wall and pointed at a creature in the mural that resembled the thing she had fought. "The Jiangshi are basically our version of vampires. They're undead creatures rising from the grave that feed on the life force of others. They're said to have been around since the Qing Dynasty, hence the magua jacket."

"I've been dealing with vampires for a while. These were something very different."

"You are right about their joints. They get their name from it. Jiang loosely translates into 'hard' or 'stiff'." He pointed at creatures on the wall that appeared to be leaping through the air. "They're known as 'hopping vampires' because of it."

"Yeah, that looks like them." She slipped off the stool and moved closer to the mural. "What are their weaknesses? How do I kill them?"

"I have never fought one myself." Zhang moved back behind the bar, pulling a book out from under the counter and flipping to a page. "I just have rumors. Some of them pretty wild."

"Most rumors have some basis in fact." She went back to the stool. "Let's hear them."

He ran a finger down the page. "They're supposed to be afraid of their reflection. It might have to do with them seeing the reality of their situation. Also, items made from the wood of a peach tree."

"That's rather specific." She sipped her drink thoughtfully. "Any peach trees around here?"

"Not in this area of the country." He looked down at the book again. "Hooves of a black donkey, blood of a black dog, vinegar, or a rooster's call all are supposed to scare them off. They're not supposed to see you if you hold your breath. If you drop a bag of coins, they're supposed to be compelled to pick them up. And they're supposed to be vulnerable to brooms, axes and fire."

"I can work with those last two." She thought. "But I didn't have any of that earlier and he crumbled to pieces. Any ideas?"

"Reflection off the glass?" Zhang scanned the book some more. "Wait. This might be something. Jiangshi are often described as having a sealing spell on a paper talisman hanging from their forehead. Maybe the tattoo you described was a more permanent replacement for the talisman."

Vampirella nodded. "And when I put his face through the glass, his skin got cut up. That must have broken the spell. causing him to revert to his natural state."

"In this case, a very old corpse that would've completely decomposed by now." He closed the book. "Damage the spell and drop the creature. Pretty straightforward."

She smiled. "I can definitely do that with an axe or fire."

Vampirella finished her drink and got to her feet. "I appreciate the information. Now I need to go find someplace to get a shower. I feel like I have Jiangshi dust all over me."

"I've got a guest room upstairs. It's small, but it has a bed and a shower." He took her empty glass and started to wash it. "You're welcome to it."

On her way towards the door, she looked back at him curiously. "I come in here looking for answers, you give them without asking for anything in return. Now you're offering me a place to stay. Why? What's in this for you?"

"I'll give you two reasons." He walked out from behind the bar. "When I was twelve, I saw my first ghost. Turns out it was the spirit of a woman that overdosed on the heroin my mom sold her. That was kind of a life-changing experience and made me dive into the supernatural world with both feet. I eventually found someone to help exorcise her from the house. By then I was hooked. In that world you're a rock star. Having you stay here would be one of the coolest things to ever happen to me."

She suppressed a smile. "And the second reason?"

"As you said earlier about rumors, there's usually some basis in fact." He walked over to stand in front of her. "Myths tend to be the same way. I have studied everything I could get my hands on and Xuè Lóng doesn't come up often, but when he does, the stories are horrific and cataclysmic. If there is even the tiniest chance that these cultists are really going to try and bring him back, then I want to do whatever I can to make sure that doesn't happen."

Zhang stood up straight, looking right at her as if presenting himself for duty. She didn't know this man or if she should trust him. She knew she should just leave, find her own place and worry about this on her own. Every person she trusted was someone that could betray her. Then again, she could put him under her control and see if he was telling the truth. She decided not to do either. There was something oddly sincere to him. And she really needed to rinse off the dust.

"Okay, show me the room."

He gestured towards the door at the back. "Right this way."

She looked around the room again. "Wait. I meant to ask. Where are all your customers?"

"Oh, right." He giggled a little to himself. "I got a call from a friend saying that a giant bat-like creature was seen flying over the city. I sent everyone home and was about to close up early to go see if I could find it when you walked in the door."

He opened the door for her, but she stopped and looked back at him. "And the bottle of blood under the bar?"

"I have a variety of things down there, just in case." He shrugged. "You never know, right?"

"You mean a monster hunter's kit? A bottle of blood, holy water, maybe some silver bullets?" She headed up a flight of stairs towards the second floor.

"Don't be silly." He followed behind her. "There are no werewolves in China. The creatures we have here are much more interesting."

CHAPTER FOUR

From above, Jincan watched the raven-haired lady in the overcoat go into the bar. Having trailed her from the Waterfront, she'd hoped to figure out how she fit in with the Jiangshi. Was she part of the Servants of the Blood? Could she be the mysterious leader that Jincan had been trying to discover for far too long? She thought about heading down to the street and going inside to see why the woman was there. But she'd come prepared for a fight, not subterfuge. Her black and gold outfit was custom made for her needs when in battle but would stand out like a beacon in a place like Shanghaied. It was best for her to move on. She had another stop she wanted to make that evening, anyway.

She reached into the pouch attached to the right side of her belt and retrieved the vial of blue liquid. She popped off the top and drank it down. Placing her palms together, right hand fingers up, left hand forward, she focused on her chi and called upon the Spirit of the Rabbit for speed and grace. She felt the essence surge through her body. Her legs suddenly wanted to run, needed to run, and she set them free. She raced forward, increasing her speed then leaping from the building, over the crowded street and onto another rooftop. Her legs moved differently now, pushing off and landing in stride, carrying her across the roof and into another leap.

Her path took her south, out over Victoria Harbour. She rode through the Cross Harbour Tunnel on the top of a semi-truck before finding her way to the Hong Kong Cemetery. Hopping the wall, she moved along the brick pathways until she found the spot she was looking for. There she thanked the Rabbit Spirit for its assistance. With its essence departing, she had to rest a moment from the exertion. She retrieved a small, circular piece of jade from the pouch on the back of her belt, then sat on the ground with her legs crossed and began meditating. She focused her mind on the image of Meili, a member of her bloodline who had died at a young age during the First Opium War. The young girl's spirit had helped guide Jincan a few times. She hoped it would be able to help her again.

"You've returned." The spirit of a young Chinese girl of no more than ten rose up from the ground. "I hoped you would."

She smiled at the spirit. "I have, and I hope you can help me again."

"I'll try." The spirit of Meili giggled. "Did you bring me something?"

"Of course." From a small pouch on the front of her belt she retrieved a handful of hard candies and placed them on a jade disk before setting them on the ground in front of her.

The spirit dropped to its knees, scooped up one of the candies and tossed it into her mouth. "I like it when you come to visit. It gets really boring around here with no one to play with."

"I will try to visit more when we can just play. But right now I need your help. Have you heard anything about the Jiangshi?" She tried to keep the questions simple. "Or anything about someone new to the area?"

Meili stopped as she was about to put another candy in her mouth. "Do you mean Xuè Lóng? There's lots of talk about him."

"What are they saying?"

Jincan had spent many years of her life tracking Jiangshi with no mention of the Blood Dragon in all that time. Now there was suddenly a connection between her quarry and the cultists that worshipped Xuè Lóng. She'd had no luck in figuring out how they were linked. The one lead she had was a safehouse in the Waterfront. All she'd found was that strange woman leaving an empty apartment. Jiangshi were solitary creatures, hunting and hiding on their own. It made no sense that they would be associated with a group of humans unless there were bigger forces at work.

The spirit looked to be in deep thought. "He found something. No, that's not it. He chose something. He's ready to return and he's chosen his... I think they said vessel."

"Do you know when this will happen?"

The child's spirit shrugged. "Nope. But it seems like it will be soon. Why else would everyone be talking about it?"

Jincan eagerly leaned in. "Was there anything else? Did they say where he would be returning or what or who is the vessel?"

The spirit shook her head and grabbed another piece of candy. It was possible that the dark-haired woman was Xuè Lóng's chosen vessel. But why would he choose a Westerner? And what made this the time for his return? She had more questions than her departed descendent had answers. She would have to look elsewhere for information.

"Will you keep listening?" She smiled at the little girl. "And I will come see you again in a few days."

"I will. And remember to bring more candy."

She was about to say goodbye as Meili reached for the last candy, but the little spirit stopped and glanced up, fear washing across her face.

Meili stood quickly, forgetting her treat. "You have to go."

Jincan got to her feet and looked around. "Why? What is going on?"

"You weren't supposed to know. They're very angry." The spirit began to fade. "I'm sorry."

There weren't many things a spirit feared, because there were few things that could hurt them. They could be exorcised, captured by certain magical items or banished by destroying their bones. Other than that, they were safe from the material world. What they weren't safe from was other spirits. And what made it worse was that those spirits could affect those in the mortal realm. How they did that depended on the type of ghost they were, which in turn depended on what type of person they had been in life. Jincan had been studying the supernatural long enough to be able to tell the different spirits apart and know what they could do. None of which she wanted to deal with at that moment. She ran for the front gate.

She moved quickly along the path, the grounds too full of tombstones and statues to cut through with any speed. There was an eerie silence to the cemetery as she ran, nothing but the sound of her footfalls and breathing. No passing cars, no crickets. It felt like there was nothing else in the world at that moment.

And that was when she saw them. Two spirits appeared in front of her. The first was once a large man. Now his skin seemed to have rotted on his bones and she could see the very ground around him decaying. A Pestilence Ghost for sure, which meant he'd harbored grudges in life. To the side of him was a female spirit that seemed to be thinner, less corporeal. She must have been an arrogant woman in life as she was left as a Hungry Ghost in the afterlife.

Jincan stopped running and thought about turning around, but the hairs on the back of her neck stood as a hot, dry wind blew against them. A glance over her shoulder showed another male spirit, a man who must've lived his life in pursuit of carnal lusts. It left him a Drought Ghost. The pressure from the wind increased so much it knocked her off her feet and sent her tumbling forward. Pestilence moved toward her, reaching out with his diseased touch. She twisted her body, putting her feet in front and using her momentum to vault over the head of the large spirit and land safely out of his reach on the other side.

With her right hand, she grasped the hilt of her jian and pulled the ancient short sword from its scabbard. Like all good weapons, this one had a name, Shi Hun Zhe, the Soul Eater. Its enchantment caused it to exist in all realms at once and thereby glow when spirits were around. She stepped forward quickly, swinging the bright blade towards Pestilence.

The large spirit retreated into the field of concrete grave markers. She tried to pursue but couldn't catch her breath. The air around her had turned thick like smoke, but it didn't smell right. She found her nostrils filling up, but no oxygen reached her lungs. She started choking on the dense mist as it began to fill her throat. Hunger was surrounding her, blocking out all the air. She would pass out if she didn't act quickly.

She held her sword out in front of her and ran for Drought. The glowing blade pointed at the center of the third ghost. It didn't run, but instead pushed forward the powerful, dry wind again. The force of the wind stopped Jincan in her tracks. It was also strong enough to blow away the gaseous form of Hunger. Jincan eagerly gulped at the heated air, easing her burning lungs. Two breaths, then a third, but she dared not delay longer. She looked around to locate Pestilence.

The decaying spirit had come around behind her and was moving in for an attack. With the fierce winds still blowing at her back and wanting to avoid the touch of decay, Jincan opened her hand, releasing the blade and letting the billowing air currents carry it. It flew out of her grasp like a bullet, right into Pestilence's chest. The glow grew brighter until she had to cover her eyes. After a second, she heard the clang of Soul Eater dropping to the ground and she knew the spirit was trapped inside the sword forever.

She scanned for the two remaining spirits. She spotted Drought some distance away. She knew he didn't need to move in to use his powers. She sidestepped toward Soul Eater, but Hunger floated forward, blocking Jincan from her weapon. She reached into her pouch and pulled out a vial of green liquid.

"Spirit of the Monkey," she cried. "Lend me your cunning, lend me your agility!" With that, she pulled the stopper out of the vial and downed the liquid in one gulp.

She felt the Monkey take hold of her and she let its spirit guide her movements as she leapt up on top of a statue of Buddha, then down onto a headstone, and then another, hooting with laughter as she went. She mentally apologized to anyone she might offend as she dashed her way across the cemetery.

Though the spirits were not constrained by the obstacles, her choice of actions seemed to have surprised them enough to give Jincan a good lead. The grounds of the cemetery extended further than she could see and she feared she would not make it out before the spirits caught her. Not far from where she was, she'd spotted a mausoleum with its door facing away from the approaching ghosts. She decided to change her tactics and made another leap, landing in front of it.

"Monkey," she murmured, "I thank you for your assistance." She pulled a vial of red liquid from her belt. "Spirit of the Ox, I beg your aid. I am in need of your strength and stamina."

She uncorked the vial and gulped down its contents and then wrapped her hands around the edge of the door and began to pry it open. She quickly completed her preparations and waited for her remaining ghostly foes.

Hunger approached the cement structure while Drought stayed a few feet back. The spirit of the arrogant woman circled around to the entrance of the mausoleum and moved inside without hesitation. From her concealed location on the roof, Jincan leapt down and pulled out a string of brass bells from inside one of her sleeves. She shook them vigorously, causing them to ring out loudly. Then she tossed them at Hunger and pushed the door shut. The tight seal would not keep the gaseous spirit trapped for long, but she hoped long enough. The bells were to wake the spirits of those buried inside, who would not be happy to find an intruder in their crypt. She wouldn't know what happened for sure, but she hoped for the best.

That left the more cautious spirit of Drought, who lingered back among the grave markers. Jincan walked slowly back towards the main path where she'd first confronted the ghosts. She kept her eyes on the spirit and he kept an eye on her. Shifting the slit of her skirt so it would show more of her bare leg, she swayed beguilingly as she walked. The spirit moved along with her but kept his distance. She unbuttoned her collar and let part of her dress fold down over her chest, revealing more of her neck. Unfastening another button, she let the material fall a little more and made sure her cleavage could be seen clearly in the moonlight. She stepped back onto the brick path and turned to face Drought. She put her hands at her sides and slowly circled around, smiling at the lustful spirit as she went.

He moved back onto the path in between her and the spot where her blade had fallen, grinning slyly. She took an exaggerated step back, then another and gestured for the spirit to follow her. He cautiously moved forward, watching her every move. She ran her fingers down her neck and along the exposed skin of her chest. A warm gust of wind blew across her, pushing her skirt further aside and forcing the top of her dress open a little more, revealing even more flesh. She smiled and gestured him closer again.

The spirit was transfixed by her.

"Drought Ghost," Jincan called to him. "Tell me your name so that I may feel it on my lips."

The ghost's voice floated to her on the hot wind. "Nianzu."

"Nianzu," she repeated after him, lingering over the name as she spoke it. The ghost leered at her hungrily, not noticing how she was moving her hand behind her back. She took two steps backward and waited as the ghost followed.

The Drought Ghost glided toward her and then stopped in his tracks, seeming confused for a moment. Then he looked down and noticed the white grains of salt in a ring around him, sparkling dimly in the moonlight.

He raised a wind inside the circle, turning to search for a weak point. She concentrated, trying to keep him from breaking through. He was far more powerful than she'd expected. Her head started pounding from the force of his assault.

She raced around him, grabbing her sword off the ground and then strode back to within two feet of the ghost.

"Even death hasn't taught you to control your desires."

In one fluid motion, she broke the salt ring with one foot while she swung the jian with the strength of the Ox. She felt a hot blast of wind hit her full force as the sword sliced through the spirit, but she held her ground. Soul Eater shone like a star for a moment and then the light faded to nothing, leaving only the steel blade.

She murmured her thanks to the Spirit of the Ox, did up the buttons on her dress, returned the sword to its scabbard and walked back to Meili's grave. The last candy was gone. Jincan bowed to the grave marker, retrieved her jade disk and then quickly made her way back to the front gate. She was outside the cemetery as the sun began to rise in the distance. She thought about leaping her way back to where she was staying, but the idea made her even more tired than she already was. She saw a cab down the street and decided to take it. As she slipped inside, the cabbie looked at her strangely.

"What?" She then remembered her outfit. "Oh, I'm part of a dance group. We have an early morning performance for students."

This made perfect sense to the driver. He smiled, took the address and fired up the engine. She sat quietly in the back, thinking about what had just happened. She'd taken on ghosts before, but never more than one at a time. And she had always tracked them down. Having them come after her was something very different. Something big was definitely in the works. But to involve both spirits and the Jiangshi? That was unheard of. Was Xuè Lóng really preparing to return? If so, how was she going to stop him?

CHAPTER FIVE

Vampirella exited the back room of Shanghaied to find the bar with a half dozen patrons well on their way to intoxication. Zhang had procured her a pair of jeans and a 'Gangnam Style' t-shirt. The clothes fit very well, which was surprising since he hadn't asked for her sizes. She pulled on her long, black coat as she worked her way through the bar. Zhang was at the end nearest the door and waved her over.

"I was thinking where you might find some more information about our zealous friends." He leaned in closer so no one else would hear. "There's a low-life a-hole that thinks he's a major player, but he's more of a weasel that people use for their dirty work. He's a displaced Brit that goes by the name Billy Bash. If he's not directly involved, he should at least know who is."

She waited as someone passed by where they were talking, then leaned in and asked, "Where can I find him?"

"I took the liberty of writing down a few of his usual hangouts." He held out a piece of paper. "He won't be hard to find. He stands 6'5", weighs over 400 lbs, and has long brown hair pulled back into a ponytail. If that doesn't make him stand out enough, he has a thin blue streak in his hair starting over his right eye."

She took the paper from his fingers and flashed a quick smile. "Don't wait up."

The first location on the list was only a few blocks from the bar. The place was called the Royal Pub & Disco, and was part of the night life on Lockhart Road. It was still early, and only a couple girls stood outside trying to get the attention of passing men. She found a spot a little over a block away where she could watch the activity. Her heightened vision would allow her to see them far better than they could see her. After a few minutes, it was obvious that the girls out front were doing more than just trying to attract clients. They were keeping track of everyone who went in and turning away some that they didn't care for. She couldn't quite make out what the criteria was for admittance, but they were definitely screening out some.

The other thing she noticed was the lack of women going inside. Maybe they didn't have female clients, but they definitely had female employees. Vampirella decided to see if there was a back entrance. She crossed the street and found an alley that ran behind a few buildings down from the Royal. For once, she could have done without her extra keen senses. The smells of various bodily fluids were a touch on the overwhelming side. She moved quietly past a prostitute taking care of her john behind a dumpster. The john tried to cover his face, but the girl didn't seem to care who watched.

She continued along to the end of the alley and walked along behind the buildings. A little way down she could see three girls behind what should've been the Royal. They were smoking and chatting softly in Filipino. She didn't know the language well enough to speak it, but could pick out enough words to recognize it.

"Good evening," she said as she approached the trio, hoping they spoke English, "I'm wondering if you could help me?"

The three girls looked at each other, then one turned to speak. "You not from here."

"Neither are you.," Vampirella replied.

"No." The girl took a step forward. "You don't belong here. Go back up town."

"You're right." She put up her hands in a sign she meant no offense. "I'm looking to deliver a message to one of your regulars. I just want to know if he's inside."

The lead girl turned to talk to the other two in Filipino then turned back. "What's in it for me?"

"Well, that depends if he's here or not."

The girl stared at Vampirella for a moment, then must've decided the possibility of money was too tempting to pass up. "Who you looking for?"

"A heavyset Brit named Billy Bash."

The name hadn't finished coming out of her mouth when all three women rolled their eyes. "He's not here. He not allowed to come back. Ever. We get all kinds in here. They ask for some real sick stuff. He's the worst. Forget your business with him and go home."

The women started talking to each other again in quick back and forth sentences. She couldn't tell what they were saying, but the tone and mannerisms were clear. They really didn't like Billy Bash and she believed he wasn't inside. She put together the rest of the cash that she had taken and gave it to the girl who had been speaking to her.

"Thank you for your help." She then retreated back the way she'd come.

The girl shouted after her. "Take my advice. Stay away from that pig."

The second name on the list wasn't a name at all, just an address. It was a few streets over and the crowds were starting to pick up. Vampirella studied the street, looking for the quickest route. Most of the buildings in the area were two or three stories high and the streets weren't particularly wide. She'd be able to move much faster with a few leaps between rooftops than she could trying to push her way along packed sidewalks. She ducked into an empty alley and hurried up a fire escape unseen.

She made a couple of leaps and was heading for a third when she got the distinct feeling she was being watched again. She didn't like that at all. She decided to change course slightly, running towards a building that was a story taller than the one she was on. She sped up and pushed off hard, the strength of her legs propelling her across the distance. She hit the wall a few feet below the roof, her claws biting into the brick. She began to climb, tugging one hand free and moving it up to where she drove her claws into the hard surface again. Making quick work of the last few feet, she flipped onto the roof and ran the short distance to the middle, where she couldn't be seen from the building she'd jumped from. She then ducked behind some venting and waited to see who was following her.

She waited over five minutes and no one appeared. Her instincts were usually dead on. Had someone been following her and figured out what she was doing? Anything was possible. She waited another minute, just in case, then got back on her path. She kept a sharp eye out as she went.

The address led her to a very busy fish and chips restaurant. It was a hole in the wall place with a dozen tables and a line halfway down the block. The to-go bags were flying out of the place. As popular as the restaurant was, it was not where she was told to look for Billy. She walked past the line of people queued for dinner and the tables full of people happily eating away. Just past the restaurant's big glass window was a solid brown door that, according to what Zhang had written on the paper, led up to a second story. This was where she needed to go.

She doubted it would be open, but she tried the handle anyway. To her surprise, it wasn't locked, and the door opened quietly, another surprise given the shabby condition it was in. Inside was a poorly lit stairwell up to a landing where a very large man stood glaring down at her. She immediately ascended the stairs, focused on the door behind the thug. At the top, she didn't even acknowledge he was there, just moved on past him, reaching for the handle. His large meat hook of a hand clamped down on her shoulder as she tried to pass.

"Show me your cash," he grunted.

Her hand snaked up and grabbed his giant thumb and turned it. She moved so quickly the brute didn't have a chance to react. Suddenly his wrist was turning, his arm followed suit and he found himself off balance with the side of his face pressed against the wall.

She leaned in, glowering at him. "Never put your hands on a woman. Do you understand?" She twisted his thumb more and a look of pain raced across his face.

"Yes, ma'am! I'm sorry!" He let out a whimper as she held him there for another few seconds. Then she released him with a push, sending his forehead back into the wall with a thud. She then straightened her coat, opened the door and went inside.

The room above the restaurant was filled with gaming tables. She saw poker, mahjong and a few other games going on. There were two roulette wheels set up in the far corner. There was a bar along the back wall and a good number of women dressed in traditional looking Chinese dresses serving drinks to a packed casino. She glanced around looking for anyone who fit the description Zhang had given her. She didn't see anyone, but she did notice a well-dressed man heading her way with a big smile plastered to his face.

"Good evening, ma'am." He gave a slight bow in her direction. "Can I help you?"

"Just looking for an open table."

"I have a seat at a twenty thousand dollar Texas Hold'em table and space at the wheel." He turned to stand next to her. "But we both know that's not why you are here."

He lifted his chin in a quick gesture towards the door where the big man stood rubbing his thumb and looking angry. "You got past Guo. I respect that. I would prefer to not have a scene in my place. If you tell me what you're looking for, perhaps we can handle this in a polite manner."

She had no doubt she could take on Guo and whatever other muscle the man had at his disposal. But fighting took time and what she was after was information, not a workout.

"We'll try it your way." She leaned in and said in a low voice, "I'm looking for Billy Bash."

"Ah." He motioned to her to move a few feet away, out of ear shot of the patrons. "I pride myself on the privacy of my clientele and would normally say nothing. But you're in luck. Mr. Bash is no longer welcome here, therefore I can speak freely about him."

"When was the last time he was here?"

"Guo tossed him out three days ago after we caught him cheating." He leaned in close again. "He was marking cards. And not well."

She shook her head. "The more I hear about this guy, the less I like him. Any idea where I might find him?"

"There is a bar called 'The Snake and the Rabbit.' I'm told there are a lot of ex-pats there and Mr. Bash is a regular." He smiled. "If that is all, I do have that seat at the poker table if you're interested."

"Another time." She smiled back.

Crossing back to the door, she found Guo waiting there holding it open for her. He kept his head down, not making eye contact. She curtly thanked him.

"Have a nice evening," he said, his voice a low rumble as she made her way out of the building.

Vampirella found The Snake and the Rabbit easily enough. It was the most British looking place on the street. A carved image on a wooden sign hanging over the door depicted a rabbit on its hind legs fighting for its life as a snake wrapped itself around it. The front window of the bar was styled similarly to some London pubs, with a wooden grid breaking it into smaller sections. She moved casually toward the window, hoping to take a look inside. Before she could even get close enough, a big man came waddling out the front door and stumbled along the sidewalk away from her. His ponytail swung back and forth along his thick back and she could just make out a streak of blue cresting over the top of his head.

She followed after him for a few blocks as he staggered along, occasionally bumping off the wall or a passerby. She had to slow her natural stride down for fear of passing him. She waited until there weren't many people around and there was an alley opening ahead. She sped up enough to be beside him at just the right spot, then she bumped into him hard enough to force him to shamble off to the side into the dark opening. His momentum carried him halfway down the alley before he stopped and realized he was off course. He tried turning around only to find her standing directly in front of him.

She grabbed him by the shirt, lifting him a few inches off the ground, and pinned him against the wall. "Billy Bash?"

He glanced around slowly from side to side, not sure what had just happened. "That's me."

"I'm told you would know where I could find the Servants of the Blood." She stared up directly into his face.

"Who told you that?" He looked down at the ground. "You're bloody strong."

She turned and tossed him across the alley into the opposite wall. The big man's back hit against the bricks and then slid down leaving him sitting on the ground. He tried to reach around to his back.

"Ouch. That hurt a lot." He looked up at her. "What's wrong with you? You could've asked nicely."

She squatted down in front of him and lifted his chin, forcing him to look at her. "I have been asking nicely all night. And what I've been hearing is that you're a low-life piece of trash that's been banned from brothels and illegal gambling halls. I was nice to the prostitutes that called you sick. I was nice to the man you tried cheating. I don't feel like being nice anymore. Now tell me what I want to know or you'll be going back to England in a body bag."

His eyes doubled in size and he spurted out the words. "I don't actually work with them, but I know who does. Or rather who is helping them find places to stash whatever they're trying to stash. I was told something happened to one of the places last night and they had to find another one today. He got them set up over at Carmen's Garden. Tower 2, eighteenth floor. Please don't kill me. I really don't want to die."

She grabbed him by the shirt and yanked him up to his feet. He was shaking and clenching his eyes shut. "I'll give you one chance. Run. If I catch you..."

She didn't get to finish the sentence before the overweight man stumbled down the alley and out into the street. She scaled the building, crossing over the roof so she could watch him run. He was surprisingly agile for his size and to his credit, he wasn't screaming. She watched him run down the street and turn the corner out of sight.

That's when she got that feeling again. The feeling that she was being watched. She turned slowly. On the opposite side of the roof stood a Chinese woman in a traditional looking black and gold dress with long billowing sleeves. It was the type of outfit you could see in many places in the city that focused on the culture of the nation. Unique to the outfit was the sword hanging off her hip and the waist cincher belt that had a row of pouches around it. All that aside though, what stood out the most to Vampirella was the look in the woman's eyes. She knew that look all too well. That woman was looking for a fight.

CHAPTER SIX

The bright light of the almost full moon shone down over the rooftops of Hong Kong. Vampirella had gone out that evening to find out more about the Servants of the Blood, a task that proved to be time consuming but not difficult. Having secured a new lead on the cult, she was ready to move on, only the woman across from her appeared to have other plans.

"What do you want?" She took a step forward and casually unbuttoned her coat.

"I thought about asking you some questions, but I think you'll just lie to me." The woman in the black dress took a few steps, circling towards the right. "I've learned honesty comes easier after defeat."

She mirrored the woman's movement, keeping the distance between them. "That's funny, my opponents usually just end up unconscious or dead."

As she moved, Vampirella slid off her coat and let it fall behind her. She could fight in anything, but she preferred the freedom her sling suit afforded her. She grasped the neck of her t-shirt and gave it a tug. The seams pulled apart, thread snapping in multiple places. She opened her hand and the shirt fell to the ground. She then extended the claws on her index fingers. She ran the sharp points along either side of her tight jeans. She grabbed them by the waist and yanked them away from her legs with little effort. She tossed the denim aside and was ready for battle.

Her opponent kept her distance, retrieving a small vial from one of her belt pouches and drinking the contents. She then stood perfectly still, her arms at her side. Her head was slightly tilted and she watched silently as Vampirella removed her clothes.

"Had you asked, I would've given you time to take them off without destroying them," the woman finally said.

"That's okay, I prefer the more dramatic approach." Vampirella charged forward, covering the distance in three long strides then throwing a right cross towards the woman's jaw.

She hoped surprise and her inhuman speed would be enough for a quick knockout. It wasn't. The woman shifted right and delivered a palm strike to Vampirella's exposed wrist. It didn't hurt, but it knocked the punch well off its mark. The woman brought up her left hand, there was a loud snap and a bright light flashed. Vampirella had just turned towards the sound when the light went off, screwing up her vision.

Not fully blinded, she was definitely distracted, and the woman moved in quickly. A hard kidney punch to her left side and another to the left temple had Vampirella staggered. The woman followed with a round house kick to the head, but Vampirella was able to block the leg with her left forearm and then connect with an elbow to the woman's cheek. They both took a few steps back to regroup. Each had underestimated the other.

The woman rolled her neck as she circled around again. "Do you have a name?"

"Vampirella." She mirrored the woman's movements. "You?"

"You may call me Jincan." She stopped and gave a slight bow.

Vampirella rubbed her eyes, trying to get them back to normal. Jincan was there when she moved her fingers up to her face, but was gone when she pulled them away again. Stunned that the woman could move so fast, she turned to try and find her only to get an elbow across the face. The blow was hard and twisted her body towards the ground. She didn't fall, though. She refused to. She caught herself and stood back up straight.

Jincan was backing away with a smile on her face. "That one hurts, doesn't it?"

She couldn't believe it. This woman was playing with her. Teasing her. "I've had worse. I thought this was going to be a fight?"

The smile melted from Jincan's face. She simply nodded and charged. Her right hand moved quickly, throwing something to the ground in front of her. There was another pop, but no light this time. Instead a cloud of thick smoke billowed up from the ground, quickly filling the space between the two women. Vampirella closed her eyes and listened. She picked up the sound of a heartbeat to her left, getting closer. She shifted away, waited until it passed, then did a leg sweeping kick in the direction of the noise. She was rewarded with a satisfying thud.

There was no wind that night, so the smoke hung over them like a blanket. The woman was back on her feet and moving in again. Vampirella wasn't sure how Jincan was locating her, but she continued to shift out of the way, then delivered another blow through the obstruction. This time she kicked out higher and caught her opponent chest high, again sending her to the ground. She followed up by dashing towards the sound and grabbing Jincan by the arm. She then braced herself and used her strength to hurl the Chinese woman out of the smoke, through the air and crashing down hard on the next rooftop over. She leapt out of the smoke herself and landed just a few feet away from her foe.

Jincan was quick to rise, but she appeared to be favoring her left shoulder. Vampirella guessed that the throw hyper-extended the joint. She had another vial in her hand that she quickly drank. Not knowing what they were, Vampirella didn't want to wait and find out. She charged the woman, targeting the hurt limb. The woman effortlessly leapt over the charge with a flip in the air and came down with both feet on Vampirella's bare back. The blow and the woman's weight slammed her down hard. She flipped over quickly, trying to grab the woman by the leg, but her opponent somersaulted out of range.

Vampirella scrambled to her feet and got into a defensive stance. She had already underestimated her opponent and then tried to compensate with her strength and speed. But rushing her attacks left her vulnerable and she now knew better. She was trained better than that. Too many fights against lesser opponents had left her cocky. No more of that, she vowed.

Jincan crossed her arms over her chest, the long sleeves hanging down past her hips. She mumbled a few words too softly for Vampirella to hear. Then, with a big flourish of her arms, there were suddenly three of her. Each one moved into a fighting stance, but a different stance from the others. Vampirella knew this had to be a trick, but she had no idea how it worked. Before she could try to deduce what was happening, the figure on the right dashed towards her with a flying kick to the head. She instinctively ducked under the kick by dropping to one knee. The figure on the left dove at her, forcing Vampirella to spin away, landing on her hands and knees. She glanced up just in time to see the third figure's boot swing up towards her face. She pushed back onto her haunches, watching as the bottom of the boot sailed past, less than an inch from her face.

She dove forward onto her right shoulder and rolled with the momentum. Her back slammed into Jincan's opposite leg, the one all her weight was on. The force took the woman down, slamming her hard against the ground where Vampirella continued to roll and brought her elbow down into her opponent's chest. There was a crack. At least one rib fractured. Jincan didn't hesitate, sliding out from under Vampirella and getting back to her feet. She spun around and ran towards the edge of the roof, leaping off into the night. Vampirella jumped to her feet and ran after her.

She got to the edge just in time to see Jincan land on a balcony across the way and enter the building. She made the same jump, landing firmly on the metal railing before pouncing forward through the open door. The room was dark save for the light coming in from the outside. It appeared to be an empty apartment. She could see a kitchen area with no appliances and a hallway leading towards a few bedrooms. As she went down the hall, she listened for movement. There was nothing. Ahead there were two doors on the left, one on the right, which was partially open. She reached the first door on the left and touched the handle.

Out of the corner of her eye she saw movement. An arm tossing something her way. Instinctively, she reached out and grabbed it. Her fist closed around it just as she heard a pop. A bright flash of light covered for the most part by her hand. She dashed across the hall slamming her shoulder into the partially open door. Jincan was on the other side of the room sliding open a window. Vampirella threw herself across the room, tackling her opponent and carrying both of them through the window and down the fifteen feet to the alley below.

Vampirella twisted as she fell so she could land on her shoulder and roll up, ready to fight. She watched as Jincan shot a line out of her right sleeve, a metal spike digging into the brick wall. It slowed her fall enough that she landed on her feet. The spike popped free and the line retracted back into the sleeve.

"Nice trick." Vampirella got to her feet. "Did you take a ninja course in night school or something?"

Jincan sighed. "Must every American partake in witty banter? I long for the strong, silent type."

"Oh, I'm strong." Vampirella walked towards her opponent. "And once I knock you out, there'll be lots of silence."

"You've been more of a challenge than your brethren. I can respect that." Jincan pulled her sword. "But I've wasted enough time."

Vampirella stopped in her tracks. "Wait. My what?"

Jincan glided forward, her blade slashing back and forth through the air. Vampirella turned to protect herself and was still stunned at the lighting speed of the first strike. The blade whooshed by her, inches away from her arm that she'd just moved. Another strike towards her chest had her backing away. A flash of steel towards her head made her duck and spin aside. As they moved deeper into the alley, Vampirella glanced around for anything she could use.

Two more dodges of quick strikes and she was getting near the end of the line. The alley ended in a brick wall. Out of the corner of her eye she saw a piece of rebar with a hunk of cement the size of a baseball at the end. She rolled under the next swing, her move carrying her over to her target. She grabbed the metal bar and swung it towards Jincan. She blocked the swing with her sword. The force of the impact knocked shards of cement of the end of the rebar.

The weighted end made the metal bar awkward to swing and much slower than Jincan's blade. Vampirella was still having to dodge as much as she was able to block. One such block left her off balance, an opening Jincan decided to push. She thrust forward with her sword. Vampirella went with her previous block and ran towards the brick wall. She ran up the wall and flipped over her opponent's head. Jincan stumbled forward. Vampirella landed up the alley and spun around, hurling the rebar towards the woman. The cement blob crashed into Jincan's shoulder, jarring the sword out of her hand and slamming her into the bricks.

Vampirella spun on her heels and raced towards her opponent, slamming her against the wall as she tried to turn. She jammed her forearm against Jincan's throat, pinning her in place.

"Enough," Vampirella growled. "Why did you attack me?"

Jincan struggled to reply with her neck being crushed. "Because... you're working... with the Jiangshi."

Vampirella relaxed ever so slightly. "No, I'm..."

Before she could finish her sentence, Jincan threw a handful of dust into Vampirella's face. The heroine gasped for air, her eyes shutting from the particles hitting them. She staggered back, desperately trying to get whatever it was off her face, but her eyes wouldn't clear. She could feel her heart start to race.

"What the hell is this stuff?" she demanded.

She heard Jincan a few feet away. "An ancient recipe I picked up along the way. It should be taking full affect any second."

Through watery eyes, she saw her opponent retrieve her sword. That was very bad. Vampirella had barely dodged it when she could see properly. She coughed and felt the dust rubbing like sandpaper inside her throat She could feel it burning up inside her sinuses. It stuck to her hand, but she couldn't stop trying to wipe it away from her eyes, which just made it worse. She felt herself starting to hyperventilate, her chest throbbing, her heart pounding like a bass drum. She felt her legs tremble. What had this woman done to her?

She glanced up again. Jincan was moving in. She tried to extend her wings, fly off until she could clear her head, but she couldn't concentrate enough to bring them out. She had to fight, but how? She couldn't catch her breath. She had to get away. That was the only thing that made sense to her at that moment. She had to run. As far away as she could get. She turned to face the building, jumping as high as she could. She dug her claws into the bricks. What if she fell? Jincan was down there with that sword. She pushed her claws harder until she felt blood run down her fingers. Then she reached up and did it again and again until she reached the top. She pulled herself onto the roof.

She didn't look to see where the woman was. She just ran the other way, leaping to the next roof and the next. She didn't want to look back. If she looked back then Jincan might be there, swinging that sword at her head. She had to get away. Find someplace safe. But where? She was alone in a city she didn't know. Nowhere was safe.

She kept running and jumping, making her way across the city at an amazing pace. As she moved, she felt her breathing ease just barely. Her eyes cleared up just enough for her to see where she was going. She was still afraid to stop or even look behind her. Finally, after what seemed like an entire night of running, she started to recognize where she was. A few blocks to the north was Shanghaied. She still wasn't sure about Zhang Wei, but it was the closest thing she had to a safe place. She made a quick cut to the right, and headed for the bar.

CHAPTER SEVEN

Vampirella threw open the door to Shanghaied and rushed inside, nearly knocking over an older gentleman who was on his way out. Unlike the night before, the bar was full of people. A few had looked up to see the commotion, but most continued on with their business. She moved towards the back wall, pushing past anyone that got in her way. She turned and put her back to the wall, She frantically scanned the crowd looking for anyone who might be a danger. Her heart was still racing like it had never done before. She didn't understand what was going on. She'd never run from a fight before. She just had to calm down and figure it out.

The people in the bar were staring at her. She could hear their whispers.

"What's wrong with her?"

"What is she wearing?"

"She's got to be on something."

"Someone should call an ambulance."

Those were just the ones in English. She could tell she was making a scene and didn't want to. But she couldn't seem to calm down. She heard a noise to the side and then felt a hand on her shoulder. She turned, grabbing the person by the throat and pinning them against the wall. It took her a few seconds to recognize that she had her hand around Zhang Wei's jugular. She immediately let him go. Everyone in the bar was on their feet, waiting to see what would happen next.

The front door opened and every head in the place turned. Jincan stepped in, sword in her hand. She moved to the center of the room. The crowd parted as she passed. Vampirella stayed back against the wall, but Zhang moved in front of her.

He faced Jincan. "Not in my bar."

"Why would you stand up for that creature?" Jincan wore a surprised expression. "Have you forgotten everything I taught you?"

"One of the things you stressed the most was that not everything is what it appears to be." Zhang took a defensive stance. "I don't know what you think she is, but Vampirella is an ally. She wants the same thing you want."

Vampirella had to force herself to not bolt for the door. She wasn't sure what was going on, but Zhang obviously knew the woman she had been fighting. The two were just staring at each other in silence for what seemed like an eternity. Then the woman put her sword away and took a step back. Zhang started talking to his customers in Chinese and a few of them headed for the exit.

He then switched to English. "I'm closing up. Everyone out. Come back tomorrow and your first drink is on the house."

There was a lot of grumbling, but everyone made their way out of the building. Zhang kept himself between the two of them. Once the bar was empty of customers, he turned and calm spoke to Vampirella.

"Relax." He spoke with his hands up where she could see them. "Everything is going to be fine in a minute. Just come with me."

"I'm watching you," she said to Jincan as she moved along with him.

He led her around the bar to the sink and turned on the water. "Rinse your eyes and mouth as best you can. Then use some napkins to blow your nose a few times."

She did as she was told while Zhang turned to face the other woman. He gestured for her to take a seat. She hesitated but finally sat her sword on the bar and slid onto one of the stools. Vampirella vigorously washed her face and eyes, rinsed her mouth a dozen times and did her best to clear her sinuses. When she looked up finally, Zhang had poured her a glass of blood. She drank it down in one swig and he filled it up again. Her heart was beating normally now. She no longer felt shaky.

"What did you do to me?" she demanded.

Jincan sat silent.

Zhang shook his head then spoke. "She used a mix of herbs and toxins to stimulate certain chemical responses in your body. You can call it a fear dust for lack of a better term. She used it on me a few times while training. I'll be damned if I know what's in it."

She stared at the bartender and then the black and gold clad woman. Something didn't seem right. Zhang looked like he took care of himself. His hair was perfect, his suit well-fitted and he was clean shaven. Taking in the gray hair at his temples, she'd put him in his mid-forties. Jincan on the other hand moved like someone with years of training and experience, but physically couldn't be more than mid-twenties. If there was a two-decade age difference with Zhang looking to be the older, how was it that he kept saying she trained him?

Zhang looked at Jincan again. The woman remained silent. He turned back to Vampirella. "Can you tell me what's going on? How did you two even meet, let alone appear to be fighting?"

"I think she's been following me for a while." She glared at the woman. "I finally found Billy and got him to talk, next thing I know you friend attacked me for no reason."

Jincan glared back. "You're working with the Jiangshi. That's the only reason I need."

"I told you you're on the same side." Zhang grabbed a bottle of whisky and poured himself a shot. "Vampirella came here after she heard that the Servants of the Blood were up to something. Why would you think she was working with the Jiangshi?"

"I was led to an apartment where four of the undead were supposed to be. I find her there instead."

"And you assumed I was a bad guy?" Vampirella shook her head. "I'd just finished smashing one of them into dust. I guess you missed that part."

Zhang threw back the alcohol and poured himself another. "Ladies. I have worked with one of you and I know the other by reputation. The apartment was a safe house for the cult. She got the information from..."

He looked to Vampirella. "One of the cult members before I let her get sucked out of a jet."

"Right." He paused for a moment then turned to Jincan. "And you went there because..."

"The spirit of my familial descendant told me I'd find the undead there." She stated this as a matter of fact.

"Right." He took a long, slow breath. "What we have here is a failure to communicate. You are both loners, but you are now investigating the same situation. Wouldn't it make sense to put this animosity aside and at least compare notes so you don't bump heads again in the future?"

The two women sat quietly for a moment, eyes locked. An exasperated Zhang took another swig of whisky then cursed under his breath. "And they say men are bad."

"Fine," Jincan spit out. "I'll tell you what I know. But if it turns out you are working with the Jiangshi, I will see you destroyed."

"Fair enough." Vampirella nodded. "And if you try to use that dust on me again, I will kill you in such a way your familial descendants will have nightmares."

Zhang clapped his hands loudly. "Oh good. We're all friends now."

It took a few minutes for Zhang to lock up the bar for the night. Once done, he had the women move over to a table where they could sit and talk. Jincan took the side further from the front door, where she could see if anyone came in. Vampirella took the opposite side of the table, but turned her chair to put her back against the sidewall where she could keep an eye on both doors and Jincan. Zhang smirked and sat at the end of the table where he could keep his eyes on both women, the two most dangerous things in the room.

He looked at Jincan first. "Vampirella is a vampire, but not a Jiangshi. She's spent her life trying to rid the world of vampires and other supernatural creatures. She's definitely one of the good guys... I mean gals."

Jincan looked at the woman across from her. She still appeared to be skeptical, but her shoulders relaxed just a little and her hand slid a few inches away from the hilt of her blade. Vampirella shifted a bit in her chair, never enjoying being the center of attention.

Zhang turned to look at her. He cleared his throat and began, "After my encounter with the ghost I told you of earlier, I went looking for more information on the supernatural. But I knew I wouldn't find it in bookstores or libraries. I began chasing rumors that were only told at bars and in back alleys. Stories of strange creatures attacking innocent and not so innocent people. I did this for a few years. In some of the stories, I heard about a woman who came to help. A magical woman that could fight off those creatures. I stuck with it long enough until I found her. She was on the hunt for a spirit going after children.

"I found her at an orphanage. The spirit was a child itself and was lonely, looking for other children to play with. But when the real children got frightened, the spirit got angry and would hurt them. Jincan found a way to communicate with it. Made it understand that what it was doing was wrong and got the child a proper burial and peace." He looked at Jincan affectionately. "I followed her around through the whole thing until she finally agreed to train me just so I'd stop bugging her."

She smiled and blushed just slightly. "You weren't that much of a bother. And it was time for me to pass on some of my knowledge."

Vampirella leaned forward in her chair. "I have one little problem with your story. You keep talking about her training you, but you look old enough to be her father."

Zhang feigned offense to the comment. "I'm sorry we can't all be supernatural creatures who never age. I'm doing my best here."

"You know what I mean." She waved off his overacting. "How can she be such a highly trained warrior yet look like she's just out of college?"

"She is at the same table as you. Please address your questions about me to me." Jincan said sternly. "As for my age, I've been alive for more than six centuries. I no longer keep specific track of years."

Both Vampirella and Zhang were surprised by this revelation. "I never knew you were that old."

She glanced at her former student. "You never asked."

"Well, no." He rubbed the back of his neck. "You're not supposed to ask a woman her age."

Vampirella turned in her chair to face Jincan now. She stared at the woman intensely for a moment as she processed this new bit of information. "You're human. Completely human. I don't pick up any sense of the supernatural on you. And I've been around magic users before. They tend to almost crackle with energy. There is an aura of power around you, but nothing on that level. You are obviously a trained fighter, but some of the things you did back on the rooftops was a combination of things that I couldn't quite figure out. So, what are you and how have you been alive so long?"

"That's rather blunt," Zhang protested. "Jincan doesn't have to answer you anymore than you have to tell her your history."

Jincan put a hand on his arm. "It's all right. In this case, my history could be relevant to what we're dealing with. But before I tell you, I have to know I can trust you. And while Zhang vouching for you is a good thing, for what you want to know, I have to be sure."

Vampirella was now genuinely curious. "How exactly would I show you that?"

Jincan reached into one of her pouches and pulled out a small ivory bowl about half the size of a grapefruit. Inside the bowl there was a symbol carved into the bottom that looked like an overhead view of a maze. Chinese writing edged the inner lip of the bowl while the outside of it was smooth without a single blemish. She slid the bowl over to Vampirella.

"I would need some of your blood," the woman said.

Vampirella was taken aback by the request. She'd known magicians and wizards that could do horrible things if they had a single drop of your blood. She was about to decline but thought about it more. She had just asked the woman to reveal her power. Someone she was just fighting not long before. And Vampirella had made the request without a second thought. Knowing the source of someone's power can could give clues to how it worked and how it might be defeated. Not very different than what the woman was asking.

She turned to look at Zhang. She'd only known him for a day, but he seemed genuine. Gave her a place to stay, a lead to follow and immediately jumped in to protect her when the dust was affecting her. He trusted this woman and she felt like she could trust him.

She extended the claws on her left hand and used her thumb to break the skin on her forefinger. She let a few drops of blood fall into the ivory bowl. The drops pooled together to form a circle at the bottom about the size of a dime. She glanced up at Jincan, who nodded her approval. She moved her finger away, took a napkin off the table and put pressure on the wound so it would stop bleeding.

Jincan slid the bowl back in front of herself, took out a pin and coaxed a drop of her own blood into the bowl. She then took it in her hand and swirled it around six times before putting it back on the table. Vampirella glanced over and watched as the little pool of blood started to move on its own, elongating into a thin line and then moving through the maze symbol on the bottom of the bowl. It was very odd to watch as the line of blood moved around the corners like a rat searching for the hidden cheese. A few seconds later the line trailed out of the maze and up the side of the cup. It circled around the edge, just under the carved letters, until it reached one that looked like a hat with two legs underneath and a cross on top. The line of blood collected together into a pool once more and clung to that spot on the cup, defying gravity.

"Neat trick." Vampirella stared, trying to figure out how the blood was holding in place. "What does it mean?"

"It means I believe you." Jincan leaned back in her chair. "I was born in the early sixteenth century during the Ming Dynasty. I lived on a farm with my family, when one day my brother was forced to go to war...."

CHAPTER EIGHT

Time moved slowly after Fan left. Hua's mother cried most mornings after serving breakfast for one less person. Her father pushed himself too far trying to do all the work that needed doing. Hua tried to help where she could, but she did not have the strength or stamina of her brother. It was a struggle, and she watched as Fan's absence took a toll on the family.

Harvest season had come and gone and winter was fast approaching the morning Hua heard the rider approaching. She was outside tending to the chickens, collecting the eggs and putting down fresh feed. Her father was repairing the wheel on one of their carts. The hammering made it difficult to pick up the sound of the hooves upon the road until the rider was almost at the house. When she finally heard it, her heart began to race. Hua ran towards the sound, certain that when she turned the corner she'd be staring at her brother, sitting proud in his saddle, a smile on his face. She flew past her father, who stopped hammering and heard the noise for the first time. He got up to follow.

She turned the corner and stopped dead in her tracks. The rider was not Fan, but a dust covered soldier with a leather satchel swung over his chest. He looked as if he'd been riding for days, but his expression was more than just someone who was tired. He saw Hua and lowered his eyes. The joy she had felt at the idea of her brother returning was quickly replaced by fear. She couldn't move. Her father patted her shoulder as he walked past her on his way to greet the rider.

"Good day," he said. "What can I do for you?"

The rider shuffled through his satchel until he found a particular letter. "From the Emperor. Is anyone in your family able to read?"

Hua's father nodded. "Both I and my wife can read."

The rider handed the letter to her father, still keeping his eyes lowered.

Her mother stepped out of the house just as her father opened the letter. Hua watched as her father's strength seemed to leave his body. His proud shoulders suddenly dropped. His legs buckled ever so slightly. The hand holding the letter dropped limp to his side. Her mother leaned forward and took the letter, looking it over and letting out the most heart wrenching wail Hua had ever heard.

"I'm sorry," the rider said softly, then pulled the reins on his horse and guided it back to the road.

Hua didn't need to hear what the letter said. She knew in her heart that her brother was dead. The details wouldn't change it. Words from the Emperor wouldn't stop the tears from streaming down her cheeks. Her brother would never be coming home.

But those words were important to her father. The letter spoke of matters a young girl wouldn't think of in a time of grief, but a father would. Things like how to bring Fan's body home and give him a proper burial. The Emperor had no problem taking men from their homes, but he could not waste the resources to bring the bodies back once they made the sacrifice. That burden would fall upon the families. Another cost on top of their already heartbreaking loss.

A week had passed, and Hua could tell something was wrong. Her parents whispered to each other in tense sounding tones. Hua didn't want to pry, she didn't want to be a burden in any way. She knew the pain they were in, she felt it herself. And even though they hadn't come out and told her, she had a good idea what was wrong. They couldn't afford to bring Fan's body home and it was tearing them up.

Hua went outside so her parents could speak more openly. She walked along the dirt path towards the road. She found the spot where she stood that morning and said goodbye to her brother. A cold chill passed over her. The weather was getting cooler, but this was more than just a breeze. She was about to head back in when she saw someone walking along the road, heading her way. They didn't get a lot of travelers passing by their farm, one or two riders a week was normal. But a man alone on foot was rare. Even stranger was the bright red robes he wore.

She was curious enough to wait as he approached. As he got closer, she saw the robes were edged in black along the bottom, center and the sleeves. The man looked to be close to her father's age and very fit. He walked like someone who did so a lot. Between the robes and the way he carried himself, Hua though he might be a Taoist Priest. The ones she'd met in the past always moved like they knew exactly where they were going even in a new place.

The man approached Hua, bowed his head in respect and then spoke in a calm, even voice. "Hello, child. Can you take me to your parents?"

She didn't know the man, but it made sense to her that a priest would come to offer their condolences and check on the family after a death. She didn't feel like speaking. She couldn't remember if she had spoken at all since the rider had come. She nodded to the priest and led him to the house. There her parents greeted the man and invited him in and her mother made him tea. Once they were all seated and Hua had found a place out of the way yet close enough to hear, the man began to explain the reason for his visit.

"We were greatly saddened to hear of your loss," he started, "I can think of no greater pain for a parent than to lose a child. What you may not be aware of is that you weren't the only house the Emperor's messenger had to visit. I know of seven other families going through a similar grief as you right now. Some of them are even more devastated because they can't afford to bring their child home to be buried."

Her father took a breath before admitting, "We are in the same situation. I tried to sell off part of my land, but I couldn't get anything close to the cost of bringing Fan home."

"I am sorry." The priest's voice sounded sincere. "There may be another way. What I'm about to say will seem unbelievable, but please hear me out. As you know it is vital that a body received a proper burial if the spirit is ever to find peace in the afterlife."

He paused for a moment.

Her parents nodded their agreement. "That is why I was trying so hard to raise the amount we needed. And it's why we feel so horrible knowing we cannot."

"My order has a possible solution that would be considered somewhat unorthodox." He leaned in a little like he was about to share a secret. "We've discovered a way to temporarily reanimate a body. We can convince the spirit to return for a time."

Her mother jumped to her feet. "You can bring him back to life?"

The priest tried calming her down. "No. Not in the way you are thinking. He won't be alive as you remember him. He would merely be able to move his body once again in a manner that would allow him to find his own way home."

"What do you mean by in a manner?" her father asked.

"When the spirit departs, the body become stiff." The priest stood so he could demonstrate. "The joints no longer work as they used to. But we can show him how to move his body in a new way. It would allow him to hop great distances. Then he will be able to bring himself home where he can finally be at peace near his family."

Her father leaned back in his chair, his head shaking from side to side. "That sounds wrong."

Her mother grabbed her father's hand. "What other choice do we have? We can't just leave him there."

She held his arm tight, her eyes locked on his as if to say, 'bring my boy home.' Her father seemed hesitant. He'd already lost so much and now he had to choose something that could be called profane. Hua felt for her father, knowing what he must be going through. But she also knew there was no other choice and that he would give anything for his son to come home.

"What do we need to do?" he finally asked.

"I will be leaving in a few days," the priest explained. "My travel has already been paid for, but there are certain things I will need to guide Fan's spirit back to his body. My order will supply those items and my services in exchange for future compensation."

Her father looked at him skeptically again. "And what would that be?"

The priest put his hands on the table. "We do not wish to burden you any more than you already are by this loss. We know your family survives based on this farm and that you will need to put a dowry together so your daughter can marry into a good family. With no sons to leave the farm to, we offer our services in exchange for a promise to donate your land to our order upon both your and your wife's passing."

Her parents sat silently once the priest finished.

He got to his feet. "I know this is a lot to consider and I wish there was more time. But I have one more family to visit before heading back to my order and preparing for my travels. I will step outside for a few minutes and let you discuss your decision."

He went out, leaving them alone in the kitchen. Hua expected them to talk, to say what they were feeling. To weigh the pros and cons. Anything. Instead her father held her mother's hand as they cried. After a few minutes, he got up and kissed her mom on the forehead, then went outside and told the priest to send Fan home.

A few weeks after the first priest had come, a second one walked up their path and told them that Fan's body had been found, his spirit was inside, and he was being trained for the journey home. The priest also had a document written up for her father to sign agreeing to leave the farm to his order. Her father signed it without hesitation. The priest told them that if all went well, they could expect Fan's body to be home in a month's time.

Hua counted the days. She knew what the priest had said, that it wouldn't be the Fan she remembered. That he would just be coming home to be buried. But she couldn't help but fantasize about her brother being the exception. That he would find a way to fully control his body again and be the big brother she'd been missing so. She knew the idea was silly, but was it really sillier than the thought of a reanimated corpse hopping across the countryside?

It gave her a bit of hope, something she hadn't had in a while. It made her days easier to get through. It made her nights more difficult though, as she would lie awake listening for bells. She'd asked the second priest how they got the bodies home. He referred to them as the Jiangshi and explained that once they knew how to hop, the priest would guide them along, traveling only at night and ringing bells as both a guide for the Jiangshi to follow and a warning to those nearby that they were coming. She didn't think to ask why they were warning people, she was too excited to know what to listen for. When it got close to the time to expect him, she started staying up as late as she could listening for bells.

Two days past one month's time, Hua sat in her bed trying to stay awake but her heavy eyelids were starting to win the fight. She had drifted off twice already and could feel her head starting to droop when she heard the first bell. It was off in the distance and she wasn't certain it was a bell. She woke up enough to keep listening. A second bell rang. Her heart stated pounding in her chest. Was this really it? She climbed out of bed and found her clothes. More bells ringing. She quickly got dressed, then ran and woke her parents.

The bells kept getting closer and closer. She ran outside and watched the sky. The moon was bright enough that she felt she would see him coming. Her parents came out and joined her. The bells rang again. This time they sounded like they were just on the other side of their farm.

Her father pointed to a spot in the night sky. "Look."

She could just make out the outline of a person jumping above the tree line. She couldn't believe it. No one could leap like that, yet there it was right in front of her. She watched in awe as the person got closer, only dimly aware that the bell had stopped ringing. Another huge leap and the person landed in the middle of their field, then it sprung into the air again, arcing up into the sky then landing just a few feet in front of her.

"Fan?" she whispered.

It looked like him. The skin was paler and the face gaunter than when he had left. There was also a series of words written on his face. But it had to be him. She started forward, only to have her father's hand stop her.

"Wait here," he commanded.

Her parents walked out towards the figure. It didn't speak or move, just stood perfectly still as they got closer.

"It is you!" her mother shouted, excitement in her voice.

Hua felt elated for a split second before what was left of her life was shattered. As her parents moved to within inches of her brother, his arms shot out towards them. His fingernails were long and sharp, raking across her mother's throat, blood flying everywhere. Fan's other hand shot forward and buried his claws into his father's chest. The older man grabbed his son's arm and struggled to pull it free.

Her father turned his head and looked at Hua. "Run!"

Fan pulled his father in close and used his teeth to rip open his throat. Hua tried to scream, but nothing came out. She saw her mother lying on the ground dying, her brother drinking their father's blood. He had told her to run and she did. She ran down the path towards the road, not daring to look behind her. Once at the road, she kept running as hard and fast as she could until she couldn't run anymore. She found a place to hide beneath a fallen tree and laid as still as she could until the sun came up.

Hua made her way to a neighbor's house and frantically told them what had happened. A few of the men from there went back to her house and looked around. The found her parent's dead bodies. There was no sign of her brother.

CHAPTER NINE

Zhang slid behind the bar and filled a glass with water. He took it back to the table and put it in front of Jincan. She smiled at him and took a long drink. Vampirella leaned back and waited. She was already impressed with the way the woman fought. She was a true warrior and had some stunning tricks. But you could learn a lot in six hundred years. Zhang took his seat again and waited for Jincan to continue.

"After the death of my parents, I was sent to live with my uncle who had no time for a teenaged girl nor her crazy stories of Jiangshi. He found a woman in a local village who needed help with her teas and herbs. She was skilled at making potions and poisons that would be considered black magic by most. She knew about the type of creature Fan had become and understood my desire to free him of this curse. She was the first of many that I have called master over the years. It's through those teachers that I've come to be the person I am now." She stopped to drink again.

Vampirella took advantage of the pause. "Your goal is to find and free your brother? Then what? Bury him and go live out the rest of your life?"

"No," Jincan snapped. "I won't stop until every Jiangshi is destroyed. No one should have to see their parents killed by these hideous creatures. And no one should suffer the feeling of guilt knowing that someone you love is out taking lives. This must end."

The room fell silent. Vampirella could see the intensity in the woman's eyes and believed her. She then looked at Zhang Wei, the man she'd just met who stood to protect her. She'd come to Hong Kong on her own, but she was starting to believe she'd found some allies.

"Zhang's lead paid off." She decided it was time for business. "Billy gave up an address. A new location for the Servants. I was thinking we could go over and take a look."

Jincan nodded while Zhang got to his feet. "I'll get a map."

Vampirella turned to Jincan. "So, am I supposed to call you Jincan?"

"That is the name I've chosen for my work." She smiled. "But my friends call me Hua."

"Okay, Hua. I only have the one name, but some folks just call me Ella." She returned the smile. "I'm curious, how have you been alive so long yet still look like you're in your twenties?"

Hua suddenly looked weary. "That is a long story."

Before she could say more, Zhang returned and laid a map of Hong Kong out on the table and the three of them got to work figuring out their next move.

According to the map, Carmen's Garden wasn't far from the safehouse at the Waterfront. And it kept with the idea of hiding in plain sight. Vampirella preferred it when the bad guys set up operations in gothic looking castles in the middle of nowhere. Fewer innocent bystanders to deal with. According to Zhang, most of the castles that used to exist in the city were torn down and replaced by what he called 'glass and steel monstrosities.'

Instead of them running across rooftops, Zhang offered to drive the women to the location. His black BMW 325i was parked behind the bar and he tried not to take offense when they both decided to sit in the back seat. "You know, Kato was the badass fighter of the two."

Both women looked at him blankly. "Who?"

"Never mind." He pulled up to the front of the building. "Should I find a place to park and wait for you?"

"We'll be fine." Vampirella waved him away. "You can go ahead and take Black Beauty home."

As the two headed for the building, Zhang was pulling away, then slammed on the brakes and yelled out the window. "Hey! You knew!"

Vampirella looked back and winked.

They headed for the delivery entrance around the back. They weren't sure how reliable Billy Bash's information was going to be. The place could be empty, or it could be filled with crazed cultists armed with explosives. There was no way to know for sure without going up to see, and the last thing they wanted to do was tip them off. A quick peek around the corner showed them a single guard stationed near the back entrance. He was reading a manga and not really paying attention. Vampirella motioned for Jincan to wait, then she stepped out and strutted over to the guard post. She got within a few feet before he looked up. The look on his face went from bothered to stunned at the sight of the half-naked heroine.

"Can I help you?" he said in a heavily Cantonese accented English.

She stared deeply into his eyes. "Let me in."

The guard hit the buzzer and she pulled the door open. Jincan dashed out from the corner and grabbed the open door. Vampirella turned back to the guard, who waited with doe eyes.

"Forget we were here," she suggested. "I'm just a figure from your comic."

The guard went back to reading as the two women slipped inside. Once inside, it took them a couple minutes to find the monitor room. They hadn't done anything to alert anyone watching yet, but that was soon going to change. Vampirella was about to open the door when Jincan stopped her.

"Let me." She knocked on the door as Vampirella stepped aside.

Another guard poked their head out the door. "What?"

"I seem to be lost." Jincan pointed down the hallway.

The man's head turned in the direction she was pointing. With the other hand she had retrieved a sandy looking powder from one of her pouches. She raised it up to her mouth and blew it into the guard's face. He instantly collapsed to the floor. Vampirella wondered just how many different potions and powders this woman had.

They dragged the guard back into the room and put him in his chair. "How long will he be out?"

"An hour at least if he's not disturbed." Jincan checked the fire exit map on the wall. "The service elevator is around the corner."

They took the guard's pass key off his belt and headed for the spot on the map. They were able to call the elevator but had to use the key to select the eighteenth floor. The car jerked hard as it started to move, then ascended very slowly.

Jincan leaned in and said softly. "Bruce Lee was cute, but I preferred Van Williams."

"I only saw it in reruns," Vampirella admitted. "But he looked good in that hat and coat."

At the sixteenth floor, they split apart and stood on opposite sides of the elevator door, tucking against the side walls. They waited for the doors to open all the way before peering out. The hallway in front of them was empty. They stepped out and glanced around to get their bearings as the elevator door closed behind them.

They were standing in a hallway with offices running on either side down towards a glass door about a hundred yards away. The offices all had large glass walls, allowing them to look inside without having to open any of the doors. They were all empty. The walls looked freshly painted and the carpet had no dented areas. It looked like the whole floor might have been remodeled after the last occupants left. Whatever the Servants of the Blood were using the place for, they didn't need individual offices.

Vampirella lead the way down to the door and paused. She could just make out the form of someone standing on the other side, a few feet into the room. Once it was obvious they hadn't been seen, she shifted over to look through the glass.

The room was filled with about two dozen people. All of them were focused on a man at the front of the room who wore a blood red robe with a black stole hanging down the front, the dragon symbol stitched into it. This appeared to be their leader and he had their undivided attention.

Vampirella turned to her ally. "Give me something small to hold the door open."

Jincan reached into her pouch and pulled out an empty vial with a cork top. She pulled off the stopper and offered it. Vampirella slowly pulled the door in towards herself. She could hear the leader's voice. She slipped the piece of cork in between the door and the jam to keep it open.

"... the loss of the one Jiangshi was unfortunate, but we haven't seen anything more of the woman. There was no information for her to find at the safehouse. With any luck, it was an isolated incident and we can move forward with our plans." The man, an older Asian, spoke flawless English with a hint of a British accent.

The room he addressed was filled with people from various countries judging by looks and clothing. The cult must be more global than she'd expected.

The man's expression became even more serious. "That's not to say we're done with her. She caused the deaths of five of our brothers and sisters. That will not be forgotten. We will find her and make her pay for the transgression. But that will be put aside for now as we focus on the reason we've come together after all these years.

"Since he was banished from this world by the Jade Emperor, Xuè Lóng has been biding his time and building up his army. Generations of servants have come and gone, waiting for the time to be right. We are the honored few, for the time has finally come. Xuè Lóng has chosen his vessel and the Transit of Venus is two days from now. He will come forth and retake the world."

The servants applauded and Vampirella took that moment to slip the cork from the door and closed it quietly.

She turned to Jincan. "What do you think? Should we crash the party now?"

"Not yet." She looked into the other room. "If we go in now, we can take them out. But what about the vessel the leader spoke of? That sounds like the key to stopping this. We need to find out who or what the vessel is and where his return will be taking place."

Vampirella held up the cork. "Okay, we'll listen a bit more. If we don't get the information we need, then we can try to grab the leader and get him to talk."

She slowly slid the door open again and put the cork back into place. The leader had stopped speaking and there was a murmur of discussion going on. Vampirella risked another look through the glass door. The leader was now talking to the guard they had left sleeping in the monitor room. The guard looked a bit sheepish while the cultist was angry and animated. He gestured for the guard to leave then turned back to the room of people.

"It appears I have spoken too soon. The guard says a woman matching the description of the one from the safehouse forced her way into the building a short while ago. And she's not alone. As much as I want to know who they are, we need to get the vessel out of here and make sure we leave no trace..."

"No!" a deep, powerful voice boomed.

The surprised leader turned to face someone just out of view. "It's not safe."

Jincan grabbed Vampirella by the arm and pulled, whispering, "We must go."

Vampirella didn't move. This had to be the vessel, the key to stopping Xuè Lóng from returning. There was no way she was going to leave when she could put an end to the whole thing right then and there. Jincan tried again, stepping to the other side and pushing on the vampire.

"These two are a nuisance and Xuè Lóng wants them dealt with, now." The vessel stepped into the room. "You may take your group and leave. My guardians will deal with the intruders."

Vampirella was about to push Jincan off of her when the warrior turned and dashed through the glass door on her own. Surprised, Vampirella followed.

"Fan!"

"Hua?" The vessel appeared surprised to see his sister. "How is this possible?"

She drew her sword. "I've come to release you. To let you finally rest in peace."

The Servants of the Blood did what they were told and ran for the stairwells. Their leader seemed hesitant, but one look at

Jincan and Vampirella and he too made for an exit. Vampirella wasn't sure what was going on. She decided to stay there and deal with the one called the vessel. She could hunt down the cultists later. And she was still trying to figure out what Jincan was doing.

As the room cleared, Vampirella got a good look at the one Jincan called Fan. He appeared to be Jiangshi. He wasn't dressed like the others had been. Instead of the traditional looking outfit, he was wearing a suit and tie. But his body was gaunt, he had the same tattoo over the right side of his face and his movements were stiff and jerky. She wondered if this could really be the brother Hua was searching for the last six centuries. The odds of it being true seemed impossible.

Fan hopped back from his sister a few feet. "As amazing as it is to see you after all these years, I'm afraid I can't let you interfere."

Two large bursts of black smoke appeared on either side of him. Both women put their hands up in defense, but nothing flew towards them. Instead, as the smoke began to clear, two new shapes took form in the room. The first was a powerful, muscular figure in plate armor with a large shield and a polearm. The second was a leaner, more athletic figure in leather armor carrying two short swords. As if two men appearing out of nowhere in ancient armor wasn't strange enough, the larger of the two had the head of an ox, while the other had the head of a horse.

Vampirella looked past the two creatures and saw that the Jiangshi had fled. "The vessel is getting away."

"This can't be." Jincan appeared to hesitate.

"What?" Vampirella was ready to fight. "Who are these guys?"

"They're Ox-Head and Horse-Face."

"I could've guessed that from the way they look," Vampirella snapped. "Why aren't we kicking their asses already?"

There was confusion in the warrior's eyes. "They're the guardians of the underworld."

CHAPTER TEN

Jincan sprinted toward the stairs, trying to go after her brother Fan. She didn't get far before a powerful arm grabbed her by the throat and threw her across the room. She slammed hard into the wall and dropped face first onto the floor. The Soul Eater dropped from her hand and slid a few feet away. She was stunned and the creature with the ox-head was moving in to finish her off. He spun his polearm around to drive the point into the warrior's prone body.

As he thrust the weapon forward, Vampirella kicked out, driving the heel of her boot into the back of the creature's hand. The strike went wide, missing Jincan's head by inches.

Ox-Head's deep voice rumbled out. "Do not interfere."

"Can't help it." Vampirella shifted to a more defensive stance. "It's kind of my thing."

"So be it." The creature turned unnaturally fast and raced towards her.

Vampirella was prepared for an assault with the polearm or even a bash with the shield. She was not ready for the creature to lower its head and charge across the room like a bull attacking a matador. She was caught flat footed. Her only move was to twist her body so his sharp horns would pass harmlessly on either side of her waist. That left his thick skull to slam into her side, nearly cracking her ribs. The force of the blow combined with the creature's powerful legs carried both of them across the room and out through the picture window eighteen floors above the ground.

The two careened out over the street and began to plummet. Vampirella slid her legs up against the creature's chest and pushed with all her might. Her momentum sent her into a tumble. She forced her wings to extend out catching the updraft of wind and slowing her descent. She tucked into a dive to get control and arched around until she spotted a shorter building fast approaching. She shifted her wings to slow herself down and landed gently onto the roof. She immediately turned and looked up to see what had happened to her opponent.

The force of Ox-Head's initial move was enough to carry him completely across the street where he slammed into the building on the other side. He punched into the cement wall and found a hand hold. He shifted hands and used his right arm to punch another hole in the building a few feet over. He repeated this a few times, moving horizontally along the building and heading towards Vampirella.

She stared at the beast in disbelief. "You've got to be kidding me."

There were more important things to worry about at that moment. She hoped Jincan could take care of herself and turned her focus on where the vessel, also known as Fan, had gone. She caught sight of a van leaving the front entrance of the building. Her wings arced up and then came down with a hard push, forcing down enough air to lift her off the ground. But before she could get any momentum going, she was slammed back down to the ground.

She found herself pinned, face down on the asphalt roof. Ox-Head stood over her, one foot on each wing. His weight kept her from rolling over and if she tried to retract her wings, it was likely they wouldn't move or be torn in half. She couldn't even twist enough to try and hit him.

Somewhere along the way, he'd lost his weapon and shield. Most likely he dropped them so he could climb along the building. But not having his polearm didn't make him any less dangerous. He squatted down over her, keeping his feet firmly on her wings. He slammed his giant right fist into her back. Then he slammed the left fist into the exact same spot.

The pain was excruciating. She could take a lot of damage and could heal quickly, but it still hurt like hell. Her strength and speed were matched, even bettered by the mythological creature pounding her into the roof. If she couldn't get up, she'd have to come up with a different plan.

"My friend called you Ox-Head, not Bull-Head." She tried to turn her head to look at him. "Is that because you have no balls?"

The creature said nothing, but she felt him hit her harder. A few more hits and he would break through her ribs and start mashing her internal organs. She shifted her arms and slammed her elbows down on the roof, not enough to lift him off of her.

She started laughing. "Does everyone in the underworld know you have no balls? I'm guessing having them cut off isn't a job requirement, or your buddy would be called Gelding-Face."

The beast gave off a thunderous growl and dropped to his knees over her, still pinning her wings down. He drove his fist down into her back and she heard cracking. His shift of weight allowed her to move her wings just a little. Not enough to turn over, but she could lift up some. She used all her strength to shove up against his exposed crotch. He didn't react, just punched down with his other fist. There was more cracking.

"I was right. There's nothing there." She laughed again. "Did you try marking your territory in hell? Is that why the cut them off?"

"Shut up!" he bellowed.

Raising both arms over his head and locking his fists together, Ox-Head slammed down on Vampirella's back with all the strength he had. Pain shot through her body and she almost screamed. There was a loud thud, more cracking and then the roof beneath her gave way. As it all collapsed, and his weight was off of her, she retracted her wings, twisted and pushed herself to the side, away from the creature. They both slammed into the floor below and scrambled back up to their feet.

Ox-Head held out his arms. His shield and polearm suddenly appeared. He was ready to fight.

"That's cheating." Vampirella extended her claws.

She charged at him this time and expected him to thrust with his weapon and keep the shield up to guard his face. She wasn't disappointed. He stood squarely and jabbed the polearm forward. She dropped to the ground and slid under the attack and his shield, through his legs and sliced across the back of his calves, tearing through the tendons. The creature let out a guttural roar of pain and dropped to his knees. She bounced back up and leapt back at him, claws raking down his back. The beast turned and caught her with his shield, sending her across the room where she hit hard.

Ox-Head struggled to his feet, growling loudly. Dropping his head, he forced himself across the room, his obvious goal to gore her. But she called on her stealth speed, blurred toward him, and dove up and over this time. The creature rammed his horns into the wall where they got stuck. Vampirella jumped onto his back and sunk her fangs into his neck and began to drink deeply.

The shattering of glass brought Jincan back to focus. She watched in disbelief as Vampirella and Ox-Head went flying out of the eighteenth-floor window. She searched around quickly until she found her blade. Having the hilt in her hand made her feel a little better. Back on her feet, she wanted to head off after Fan, but there was an obstacle in her way. Horse-Face stood, patiently waiting.

"You are determined." His voice was nasal and breathy. "Come. Let's get this over with."

He swung his two short swords back and forth quickly, cutting through the air with a series of whooshes. He then turned sideways, held one of his blades at his hip, point forward. The second blade he held high, just above his head with the pommel forward. Jincan took up a ready position, her blade held up over her back shoulder.

"Are you not concerned about your partner?" She slid forward a few inches.

He did the same. "Ox-Head can take care of himself. I wouldn't expect to see your friend again."

"That's okay." She moved up again. "I just met her."

The guardian of the underworld got impatient and struck first. He brought the first sword in high in what appeared to be a feint. He let the move carry him into a full spin and then struck with the low sword as he came around. It was a strong first move against an unsure opponent. Jincan was ready for it, dodged the first strike, bringing her jian down to push the second strike away which left an opening for a palm strike. She struck hard against his muzzle, causing the creature to retreat a step.

She moved back to her ready position, keeping an eye on her opponent. It appeared he was smiling. This made her more nervous than the idea that she was going up against a creature of legends. Horse-face spun his swords, reversing the hilts so the blades ran up the lengths of his arms. He held one up in front of him, the other at his side. She'd seen a stance like this before, but with knives. Never with swords.

He stepped forward and blades started flying. Jincan did her best to block the strikes she could see, but her opponent had become a whirling dervish. His attacks where blazing fast but not lethal. She could feel as the blades cut across her shoulder, her cheek and her leg. He could've killed her if he really wanted to. Instead it felt like he was testing her limits.

He stepped back and crossed the swords over his chest. She tried to catch her breath while digging into her belt to retrieve one of the blue liquids. She gulped it down and spoke softly. "Spirit of the Rabbit, I ask for your help."

The way this worked for her was in two parts. The potion she took gave her a boost of adrenaline and speed, but only a small amount. It also prepared her for the influence of the animal spirit. That was the true enhancement. But something was different this time. Something was wrong.

"That won't help you." Horse-face whinnied. "None of the animal spirits will stand against us. Your potions are useless as well. You must face me on your own."

He held both blades in front of him, straight up. He dashed forward and struck with the right sword, stepped back, then dashed in again and struck with the left. He repeated this over and over as Jincan began to tire. The force of each blow shook her body. She cast the mirror spell, but the creature ignored the two illusions and kept focused on the real woman.

She had to change things up while she still had the strength. On his next strike, she didn't try to block it. The sword cut across her chest, slashing through cloth and skin. She ignored the pain, thrust forward with her own blade, forcing him to block it. This left him off balance and his right elbow exposed. She struck a nerve cluster at the base of the elbow with a knuckle strike. It forced his right hand open and the sword dropped. She caught it with her left foot, spun on her right and sent the blade flying across the room and out the shattered window.

"Clever." He nodded in approval. "But what have you really gained?"

He switched his remaining sword to his right hand and quickly lunged forward. Instead of blocking, she moved back. He attacked again and she backed away again. On the third thrust, she smacked his blade with her palm and stepped in as she cut across his chest.

She glanced down at the blood dripping down her dress then at his wound. "Now we are even."

"This has been more fun than I had anticipated. But it's time I end this."

He moved in at supernatural speed. If she hadn't been anticipating the move, it would've killed her. But she got up enough of a block to force his blade to just cut across her arm. With her other hand she tossed the fear dust into his eyes. She knew there would be no effect on the creature, but it would still blind him.

He swung wildly while desperately shaking his head. She rolled under his swing and waited until he was almost completely turned around. She put everything she had into one final thrust. The blade pierced the creature's side and she forced it up, towards his heart.

"No! This can't be happening!" he yelled out.

Soul Eater began to glow, softly at first. But it got brighter and brighter until she had to shield her eyes. She pulled the blade out, expecting the soul to be trapped as it had been with every other spirit she dealt with. But the sword continued to grow brighter until a wave of energy erupted from it. Jincan was knocked off her feet and the blade went flying. Every window on the floor shattered. There was the deafening sound of raining glass and then silence.

When she finally got back up, she saw her sword on the other side of the room, no light to it at all. She retrieved it and put it back in its scabbard. The body of Horse-Face lay where she had stabbed him. Except it no longer had the head of a horse. It was just the corpse of a man. One she didn't recognize.

"His buddy did the same thing to me." Vampirella's voice came from outside.

She flew in through the window she had gone out of. Jincan saw blood down the face and neck of her ally and remembered she was a vampire. She tried to cover her own open wound.

"Don't worry. I'm full." Vampirella pointed at Jincan's wound.

Jincan dug a healing potion from her pouch. "Are you okay?"

"Fine, just mad the vessel got away." Realization hit her. "That was your brother?"

Jincan drank the potion and took a deep breath before answering. "Yes. It seems laying him to rest may be more complicated than I initially believed."

"You finally found him after six centuries. Don't give up now." Vampirella looked around the office. "Though I'm not seeing anything that might tell us where they went."

"What about the thing two days from now?" The wound on Jincan's chest has stopped bleeding and the cuts were fading. "He called it the transit of Venus?"

Vampirella looked out the window at the street below. "Police are here. Let's head back to the bar and regroup. We'll see what we can find out about this Venus thing and go from there."

"How are we going to get past the authorities?" She glanced down. "There looks to be a lot of them."

"Don't worry." Vampirella spread her wings out. "I can give you a lift."

CHAPTER ELEVEN

Vampirella sat in the passenger seat of the black BMW as Zhang wove the car through morning traffic. They were headed to the University of Hong Kong where Zhang had made an appointment for them with a Doctor Fung, an observational astronomer. After they'd returned to Shanghiaed late the night before and caught the bartender up on what happened, he had gotten up first thing in the morning and started making calls. He also obtained regular clothing for both women. Vampirella was dressed in another pair of jeans, this time black, and a simple white button-up blouse. Jincan sat in the back seat wearing a blue, floral print dress. Neither of them wanted to ask Zhang where he got the clothes or how he knew their sizes so well without asking.

They reached the campus and got one of the students to direct them to the Astronomy and Astrophysics Department. They found Fung working with the radio telescopes. He was a short man with a round, happy face and hair that looked like it may never have seen a comb. He greeted them warmly, speaking first in Cantonese then switching to English.

Zhang did the introductions. "I'm the one that called you. We appreciate you taking the time to see us. These are Hua and Ella."

"Charming to meet you." He grinned with excitement. "I am always happy to help explain the ways of the cosmos. And it gives me a chance to look up from my work for a while."

"What is it you are working on?" Hua asked.

"I've been writing a paper on stellar coronal magnetic activity, which involves a lot of observation time on the telescopes." He shook his head. "Sometimes I'm not sure if it's morning or night."

"It's morning on a rather nice day," Zhang offered. "Would you like to talk to us outside?"

"That sounds wonderful." He immediately went to the door, motioning for them to follow. "Come."

Outside they found a grassy area with a table and benches. Zhang took a seat next to the astronomer while the ladies sat on the opposite side. Fung leaned back for a moment, letting the sun wash across his face. He took a few deep breaths, put his hands on the table, steepling his fingers together and sighed.

"Now, what can I do for you?"

Ella had sat directly in front of the doctor. "What can you tell us about the transit of Venus?"

"That one is surprisingly straightforward." He paused and she watched his face change from happy and friendly to wise and scholarly. "It's when the planet Venus travels between the Sun and the Earth.

"Like a lunar eclipse?" Hua asked.

Fung smiled approvingly at her. "Same concept. But where the Moon can block out the entire Sun at times, Venus is too far from the Earth and just appears to be a small disc traveling across the Sun. It can take well over six hours for it to complete.

Zhang had pulled out paper and a pen to take notes. "And we have one coming up?"

"Yes, tomorrow at 6:09 A.M." Fung looked thoughtfully. "I was planning on taking my students up to the top of the Nina Tower to watch it. But I'm told that they're having a private party booked at that time."

Zhang looked up from his notes, "What else can you tell us about the transit?"

"It's among the rarest of predictable astronomical phenomena." He started talking with his hands. "It's a pattern that repeats roughly every 243 years. They happen in a pair of pairs. The first set takes place after 121.5 years and again eight years later. The second pair then happens 105.5 years later and then another eight years. It starts again after that. Johannes Kepler was the first to predict the transits back in 1627."

"That makes sense," Hua interrupted. "I've been trying to figure out why the Jiangshi would have bouts of population growth, again a few years later and then nothing for more than a century. It's possible that they can only be created around the time of the transit."

Fung looked confused. "Did you say Jiangshi?"

"That would mean Xuè Lóng can only use his powers on Earth when the Sun and the Moon aren't looking," Zhang added.

"You're talking about hopping vampires?" Fung made a hopping motion with his right hand. "I do astronomy, not astrology."

Vampirella turned her attention back to Fung. "What were you saying about the Nina Tower?"

"It's the tallest building in the city. Eighty stories." He seemed more comfortable talking facts again. "It wasn't completed until 2006, two years after the last transit. I took my students there for the last lunar eclipse, so I figured I'd do the same this time, but as I said, it's already booked."

She turned to the others. "I bet that where they're going to do the ritual to bring back the Blood Dragon."

Fung jumped up. "There's a reason I never go outside anymore. You people are crazy."

He stormed off back to his telescopes, the others hardly noticing him leave. Zhang wrote down the name of the building along with the date and time of the upcoming transit. He then tucked the notes back into his pocket and got up from the table.

"Let's head back to the bar. I'll make some calls and see if I can find out who has the roof booked. Just to be sure it's not a different group of students on a field trip."

Hua got to her feet. "Can you drop me at my place? I need to pick up some supplies and repair my outfit."

Hua was staying at the Peninsula Hotel, one of the best in the city. But she didn't choose it for the comfort. She never stayed in the same place more than a couple of days and picked spots that were constantly busy. Places where the Jiangshi would get noticed instantly. Okay, she also liked the comfort and the room service was very good. Cost wasn't an object to her. She found that if you live long enough and invest money wisely, you could build up a small fortune. That and occasionally selling the right potion to the right person could bring in a lot of money.

Once in her room, she pulled her sword and what was left of her things out of the duffle bag Zhang had loaned her. She put the sword onto the desk in the corner. Her cincher belt was still in good shape, but the dress was beyond salvaging. She tossed it into the waste bin by the desk and retrieved another just like it from the closet. She had four more waiting if needed.

She pulled out a metal case from under the bed and opened it. Inside were the different ingredients needed to make her potions and powders. She had enough premade to restock her pouches, which was good as she was far too tired to focus on proportions and mixing things. What she really needed was a long, hot shower and a nap.

She went into the bathroom and started she water. She pulled off the floral dress and tossed it onto the sink, slid off her boots and everything else and stepped into the shower. The hot water pulsed against her bare back and she finally felt herself relax. She grabbed the bar of soap and ran it across her body. As she lathered, she felt her fingers run across each of the cuts she'd gotten from Horse-Face. Anyone looking would have a hard time finding most of them. That was the power of her healing potion. But she knew they were there. The skin just felt slightly off. And then there was the four-inch gash across her chest. It had completely closed and now looked like a white scar against her pale skin.

Why had the creature been toying with her? He had her dead to rights multiple times, yet his attacks were less than lethal, like he just wanted to wound her. He almost seemed bored. Like he was doing a chore that he didn't want to do but that had to be done.

She thought about the end of the fight. She was certain that he'd escaped Soul Eater, which wasn't supposed to be possible. It seemed her magical sword had limits. The question that really bothered her was about the other souls. Were they still in there or had they escaped with Horse-Face? She had won the sword in battle. It didn't come with an instruction manual and she'd killed the previous owner. Everything she'd learned about how it worked was through trial and error. She'd have to set aside some time in the future to try and find out more about the blade.

Hua finished up by washing her hair. By the time she was done, the room was filled with steam and she felt better. Still in need of sleep, but better. She grabbed one of the big towels from the rack and dried herself off. After wrapping it around her body, she took a second towel to her wet hair. She stepped out into the main room with the idea of slipping into bed.

She was surprised by just how cold it was. She'd expected some chill having come out of the hot shower, but she hadn't turned on the air conditioner and she was feeling a breeze on her exposed skin. She immediately went for her weapon, but it wasn't there. She looked into the seating area of her suite and found her brother standing next to the couch, holding the sword.

"What a magnificent weapon." He swung the Soul Eater back and forth a couple times. "Perfect balance. How ever did you come to possess this, Little Squirrel?"

"I killed for it." She glanced around the room looking for anyone else. "What are you doing here?"

"I can't come to visit my sister?" He feigned being offended. "What is this world coming to?"

He slipped the sword back into its scabbard and placed it on the couch beside him, in close reach. She came further into the room and stood by a chair, choosing to stay on her feet. She looked Fan over closely. He looked exactly the same as the day he killed their parents. No sign of aging, no additional scars. Even the tattoos were the same. Only the clothes he wore were different. And he'd changed them since she saw him the night before. He was dressed casually in a pair of khaki pants, a green polo shirt and a pair of brown loafers.

"Fine. You're here. What are you doing with the Servants of the Blood?"

He chuckled. "Oh, them. They're a necessary evil, really. Their order has been around for a very long time. I believe you met one of them back on the farm. He offered to bring my body home."

"Where you slaughtered our parents." Rage built up inside of her. "You drank their blood and left their corpses to rot. How could you do that?"

Fan looked away before answering. "I wasn't in control then. I had no choice. Most of my time as a Jiangshi has been spent following their orders and living off of animal instincts. Sleep, eat and kill. Hidden away from the world most of the time, waiting as Xuè Lóng built up his army."

"What changed?" She glared at him. "You seem to be in complete control now. They were calling you the vessel."

"Turns out, that's your fault." He hopped towards an open window that hadn't been opened before. "Xuè Lóng took notice of your activities over the many decades. How you were chipping away at the army he was building. And while you weren't doing any real damage, you were annoying enough for him to keep an eye on you. Eventually he realized your motivation. Your desire to free me or whatever you are planning. He decided to make me his chosen."

She scoffed. "He thinks I won't kill you to stop him? He's wrong."

"You can't kill me, my body would dissolve and you'd have nothing to bury." He shook his head. "The best you can hope for is to undo the spell that turned me into Jiangshi and take my remains home for interment. Except you don't even own that land anymore. And now that I'm his chosen, you're not powerful enough to force his will out of this body. By tomorrow he will be in complete control."

"If you're so confident I can't do anything to stop this, then I'll ask you again: why are you here?"

He crossed the room and stood directly in front of her. She wanted to back away but stood her ground instead. He reached up and touched her cheek in a loving way.

"Until tomorrow, I'm in control." He gave her a soft smile. "You have spent many lifetimes trying to correct a wrong that wasn't your fault. You haven't lived a single moment of your life, Little Squirrel. It's time for you to walk away. Put down the sword, stop chasing ghosts and enjoy what little time this world has left."

She touched the back of his hand. "And if I don't? If I choose to stay here and try to stop Xuè Lóng?"

"Then you will die painfully." He stepped away. "His return is inevitable."

He hopped up on the window ledge, looking like he was about to leave. She moved closer, her emotions mixed. She was close enough now to grab her weapon, but the thought never crossed her mind.

"They never told us how you died," she asked.

He frowned and looked out the window. "I would love to say it was in some heroic moment where I was taking out a bunch of the enemy or saving my fellow soldiers. But it wasn't anything like that. We were told to make camp in a valley about a mile back from where the fighting had been. We were to get up at first light and march into battle. But the enemy had a better plan. They left their camp an hour before dawn. By the time we were waking up, they were already on us.

"I came out of my tent, sword in hand, trying to figure out what was going on. I didn't hear the guy, just felt the point of his blade drive into my back. I dropped to my knees and he yanked his sword free. I tried to reach for the wound, but he just kicked me over. I laid there on the dirt bleeding out. I saw a few other people die before everything went black."

"I'm sorry," she said softly.

"Me too, Little Squirrel." He leapt out the window.

She thought about running after him, seeing where he went. She didn't. She left the window open and went back into the bedroom. She could feel the tears rolling down her cheeks as she slipped under the covers. Her brother came to her to try and save her life. Just as she'd been focused on trying to save him all those many years. She had a choice to make. Would she take his advice and leave? Find a life of her own somewhere. Or would she try to stop Xuè Lóng, the reason he was a Jiangshi in the first place? It wasn't an easy choice, made even harder by Fan's visit. If he'd just been a mindless zombie, things would've been simple. Or at least easier.

She curled up under the covers, thought about her parents, her brother, and she cried.

CHAPTER TWELVE

The Nina Tower stood out in the Hong Kong skyline. The name was somewhat misleading as it was two buildings side-by-side. There was the eighty-story skyscraper and a shorter, wider building that went up forty-two floors. It was designed to be the tallest building in the world, but due to restrictions in the city, the plans had to be changed, cutting off six-hundred and fifty feet from the original proposal. The tower looked like a giant obelisk in the center of the New Territories that scaled in a couple times as the building rose and had rounded corners. At the top were a series of five parallel half-arches making the top of the tower look like a Spartan helmet without the crest. It made for a very interesting silhouette.

Vampirella and Jincan arrived at the tower and entered through the lobby. It was ten to six in the morning and they expected the building to be mostly empty except for a few security guards and bad guys. They entered the lobby and made their way towards the elevators. As Vampirella lead the way, she noticed there was no guard at the front desk. The lobby itself looked like something out of an M.C. Escher painting. The wall above the bank of elevators was made up of geometric shapes all protruding out at different depths. There was no discernable pattern to the shapes, even the color of the shapes varied irregularly. She found it a bit disconcerting that someone would choose to design a lobby like that.

The light panels showed that three elevators were all headed down to the first floor. She and Jincan moved over to the one that would arrive first. They waited close to a minute before they heard the car brakes kick in and the elevator come to a stop, followed by a sharp ding. When the doors opened, they found the car wasn't empty. There were five Jiangshi starring at them and a heartbeat later, if they had heartbeats, all five rushed out of the elevator toward them.

Vampirella dove to the left, just under the strike of the first Jiangshi. She extended her claws and swiped across the creature's face. She came back with a good inch of tattooed skin, enough that her attacker crumbled into dust on the marble floor. "Destroy the tattoo and they drop instantly."

Jincan drew her sword. "Decapitating them works as well."

"That's why there was an axe in the list of things that could hurt them." Vampirella shook her head. "I knew I should've brought one."

The warrior stepped up to the two monsters charging her. She used a swing of her long sleeves to distract the first one then followed up with a sword strike to the neck. Soul Eater sliced across the creature's throat but didn't go deep enough to sever the spine. It spun away from the attack while the other Jiangshi moved in, spinning its arms like windmills. Jincan jump-kicked the creature in the chest, using the attack to push off the Jiangshi's chest and flip backwards out of range of the whirling arms.

Vampirella saw the other two move in to attack, but was more interested in the one with the partly wounded neck. She used her supernatural speed and strength to dive between the two heading towards her, somersaulted back up to her feet and leapt towards the wounded Jiangshi. In one fluid motion she grabbed it by the head and twisted. The already damaged spinal column gave way with a snap. Her boots hit the floor and she slid three more feet with the creature's head tucked under her arm like a football.

She tossed the head aside as it began to disintegrate. "Two down, three to go."

From behind her she heard another sharp ding. She glanced over her shoulder at the opening elevator doors to see four more Jiangshi piling out. "Make that seven."

"And probably a few more." Jincan pointed at the third elevator on its way to the lobby. "When they all get here, try to bring them to me."

Vampirella was unsure of her ally. "Do you have a plan or a death wish?"

"I am not afraid to die." Jincan spun to the side as a Jiangshi dove at her. She grabbed him by the collar as he passed and yanked him back with her left hand while bringing Soul Eater up with the right. The blade cut cleanly through the neck, sending the head flying across the lobby. "But I have no intentions of dying today."

Four of the Jiangshi raced towards Vampirella. She was able to block the first attacker and push him aside. The second one dashed past, raking its claws across her bare back. The third one left a slash in her thigh. But the fourth got an elbow to the nose that mashed it to pulp. Before she could deliver a second blow, the first Jiangshi turned around and attacked again. Like strafing runs by enemy aircrafts, they used their speed to get in close enough to take a swipe and then moved away as the next one attacked. Their quickness and teamwork negated her own speed and strength. She couldn't damage what she couldn't hit.

She leapt up and grabbed one of the protruding shapes above the elevators. She flipped up on top of it and tucked into a crevice created by the odd design. One of the Jiangshi jumped up after her. It grabbed the top of the shape she was kneeling on and pulled itself up. She shifted to the side in the space, revealing that, like a handful of other spots on the wall, this one was mirrored. The creature saw its own reflection and froze. It stared at itself. Vampirella didn't know what the Jiangshi was thinking, nor did she really care. She struck quickly, dragging her claws across the right side of its face, tearing away tattooed skin. She watched as the creature turned to dust and rained down on the lobby.

She glanced down and saw the other three that had attacked her were just staring at the falling dust. Off to the side, Jincan was fending off two other Jiangshi with her sword.

Vampirella called down to her. "These are a hell of a lot easier to fight one at a time."

"I don't think they're interested in waiting their turn." The warrior moved quickly, taking off one of the creature's hands.

Vampirella's attention turned at the sound of another sharp ding. "I hope your plan is ready."

She smashed the mirror behind her, grabbed the biggest shard she could and jumped down to the lobby. She aimed for one of the remaining monsters. It sidestepped as she'd expected, but she was able to bury the shard of glass deep into the Jiangshi's right eye, slicing through the tattoo. The creature crumbled, leaving the four already in the lobby and another three hopping out of the newly arrived elevator.

Vampirella sped across the lobby, stopping with her back to Jincan's back. "What's the plan?"

The warrior reached into her left sleeve and pulled out a dark blue glass ball about the size of a volleyball. "Take this, smash it on the ground when I say to."

She took the ball while Jincan pulled a second one out from her other sleeve. "Where the hell were you keeping this?"

"Don't question the magic." She held a glass ball over her head as all the Jiangshi approached. "Wait for it."

The creatures appeared to be mindless before, but Vampirella questioned that now. They were moving in cautiously, staring at the two blue spheres. She couldn't tell if they were worried or just distracted, but they approached slowly.

Jincan shouted, "Now!"

Both women hurled the objects, shattering them against the hard marble floor. Broken glass mixed with copper coins, flying around the lobby in every direction. She recognized some of the coins as U.S. pennies. Others she couldn't tell. But the effect of the loose change was fascinating. All of the Jiangshi dropped to the floor and started counting.

Jincan held her sword over one of the Jiangshi, bringing the blade down swiftly and decapitating the monster. The others didn't react, they just continued counting.

"You've done this trick before?" Vampirella asked.

"Once or twice." Jincan pointed towards the security desk. "If you care to join in..."

Vampirella looked over and saw a fire axe hanging on the wall behind the desk. She smiled and sped across the room. She grabbed the wooden handle and was back in the blink of an eye. "Shall we?"

Together they made short work of decapitating the final six Jiangshi. The whole fight took a little over ten minutes, which didn't leave them long before the transit began. It took a few minutes for another elevator car to arrive and the ride up took a few more, including shifting to another elevator to get to the upper floors.

While in the second elevator, Vampirella turned to Jincan. "What happens if the only way to end this is to kill your brother?"

Jincan looked thoughtful for a moment. "My brother has been dead for a very long time. What we're about to face is an abomination. I just hope to have enough left to give my brother a proper burial."

"Good." Vampirella turned back to the door. "The last thing I need is you trying to save him while I'm trying to save the world."

They rode the rest of the way in silence. By the time they reached the roof, it was close to the time and things were happening. A dozen Jiangshi formed a ring as big as a crop circle in the center of the roof. Inside the circle were the Servants of the Blood, each kneeling over a golden bowl. In the very center of the circle was Fan dressed in a black and crimson robe. The cultists all pulled out ceremonial daggers and slit their wrists open on both arms. They let the blood run down their palms and fingers to drip into the bowls.

Jincan pointed to a small black sphere crossing the rising sun. "We're too late."

Fan stood with his hands out wide and said a series of words Vampirella didn't understand. She noticed the bowls were all starting to overflow, and the cultists were passing out. Parts of the blood lifted up from where it had fallen, collecting about three feet above the ground. With a move of his arms, the blood spun around him, collecting together as it went. Every drop rose to join in the stream. Once it was all gathered, the blood made a sharp turn and flowed towards Fan. He opened his mouth wider than he should've been able to and the whole stream blasted into him. Not a drop was lost.

Fan cackled manically and dropped to his knees. His limbs jerked side to side and bent in unnatural directions. It was like watching him have a seizure except his body was stretching and growing with each movement. He dropped onto all fours, except his arms had elongated to twice their size. His hands grew wider, more muscular, and his skin was turning red and cracking. His nose and mouth stretched forward while his entire body added mass.

Vampirella tried to figure out where the mass was coming from. It was then she noticed that the cultists had dissolved, leaving nothing but empty robes behind. Fan had turned their bodies into particles and added them to his own shape. And that shape had drastically changed. The broken skin had hardened, turning into red scales. Sharp ridge lines formed along his spine and covered part of his head. His legs were as thick as tree trunks and a six-foot long tail had appeared out of nowhere.

He laughed again, but now his voice sounded like approaching thunder. Two boney protrusions forced their way out of his back and grew quickly. They doubled then tripled in size and spread out forming to look similar to Vampirella's own wings. A moment later the metamorphosis was complete. Fan was gone.

In his place was Xuè Lóng, the Blood Dragon.

The monster moved forward as the Jiagnshi shifted out of its way. "Now it's time to deal with the two of you."

Vampirella took off to the left only to be knocked across the roof by one of his mighty wings. She went tumbling toward the edge, just catching her foot on the lip before going over the side. Xuè Lóng moved in closer to Jincan. She appeared to be frozen with fear.

"He warned you to leave." His mouth was just inches away from her. "Your death is your own fault."

Jincan tossed a handful of black dust into the dragon's face, startling it. It took a step back. She dove to the side as the creature struggled to breath. Vampirella was back on her feet and waiting for an opening. He staggered another step and desperately gasped in air. His head flew back and shot forward again letting out a powerful sneeze. The force of the air coming out of the dragon's lungs shot one of the Jiangshi clear off the roof.

Vampirella took this moment to attack. She raced in using all her speed and swung the axe with all her strength. The blade sliced into the scaly skin about an inch, not enough to draw blood. The force of the blow shattered the axe's wooden handle, leaving nothing but kindling in the vampire's hands.

Xuè Lóng jerked his head hard to the right, catching Vampirella with his muzzle and sent her flying into another Jiangshi. The rest of the creatures stood watching their master as if waiting for orders. Vampirella untangled herself from the one she hit and got back up just as Jincan ran in for an attack. She swung her sword for the dragon's eye. He turned fast enough to force the blade to skip harmlessly along his scales instead.

She was now too close and he swiped at her with his claws. One of the points ripped across her midsection, tearing away her belt and cutting deep into her stomach. Blood spurted out of her and hung in midair. Like with the cultists, the blood collected together and magically carried itself towards Xuè Lóng's mouth. But when the blood hit him, it burned. The dragon growled in pain. It was obvious he hadn't expected that. Reflexively, his wing shot out and sent Jincan flying off the roof and plummeting towards the city below.

Vampirella sprinted across the roof. The dragon took a swing at her with his other wing. She slid underneath the attack and grabbed Jincan's belt as she went by. She had to roll to avoid a second swipe by the other wing, sprung back up and ran for the roof's edge. She forced her wings to extend out and bounded into the air.

She looked down, searching for Jincan. The warrior was falling quickly. Vampirella tucked her wings in close and dove after her. She picked up speed as she fell. Once she hit terminal velocity, she used her wings to go faster. A few powerful strokes and she was within a few feet of the falling woman. The problem was the other tower was approaching fast. Vampirella stretched out and her fingers brushed against Jincan's arm, but she couldn't grasp it.

The roof of the other building was coming up way too fast. She reached out again, this time Jincan turned slightly and grabbed Vampirella's arm. The vampire secured her grip and pulled up hard. The wind caught under her wings and slowed them some, but not enough to stop them. She cut hard to the left and pulled Jincan up closer to her. They barely sailed past the antenna towers on top of the building and into the clear air. That was when Vampirella heard the loud growl from above them.

CHAPTER THIRTEEN

The city of Hong Kong was built up as much as it was built out. Tall buildings crammed close together created a maze of obstacles for a winged woman trying to lose a dragon. Vampirella couldn't go as fast or maneuver as much with the added weight of Jincan in her arms. Xuè Lóng was unencumbered and determined to catch them. Normally she would turn and attack. She'd already done more running than she was comfortable with. If she was going to save her friend, she needed to escape before Jincan succumbed to her wound. Outrunning wasn't an option, so she tried to lose him in the buildings.

She headed north as quickly as she could. When the dragon was right behind her, she cut sharply at the last minute, making a hard left just prior to a building. The only advantage she had was her size. The dragon's wingspan was more than twice her own, which she tried to use. The monster couldn't cut as sharply but tried anyway. He slammed into the side of the building, shattering glass and bending steel. This gave her a few seconds. She circled back to the south and zigzagged around a few corners, keeping the distance she'd gained.

She flew towards a pair of masts atop the Bank of China Tower. Now in the open, Xuè Lóng was starting to catch up. Cutting between the building's twin spires, she immediately dove and headed down the side of the structure. Glancing over her shoulder she saw the dragon come through the spires with its wings tucked in, slowing it down. She banked hard to the side and circled the building. She hoped that the move would give her a few seconds out of Xuè Lóng's sight.

As they came around the building, Vampirella landed on an observation deck and pulled the unconscious woman into an alcove. She held her there and remained as still as possible. The dragon circled by and then was out of sight. She took a moment to check Jincan's stomach. The cut was deep and bleeding freely. She tore a foot off of the bottom of the warrior's dress and pushed it against the wound. As she kept pressure on the makeshift bandage, she looked at the belt that dragon had knocked off. The creature's claw went through the metal fastener, bending it and causing it to come off. With her incredible strength, Vampirella was able to bend the metal clip back into place. She wrapped the cincher belt around Jincan's waist and tightened it. The belt held and would keep pressure on the wound.

A loud whoosh of wind sounded as the dragon swooped by again. Vampirella gently laid the woman against the alcove corner. "I hate to leave you, but I'm guessing he's following the smell of your blood. Which means escaping is going to be very difficult unless I can slow him down. I'll be back for you soon."

She ran for the edge of the balcony and leapt off. Her wings expanded out wide and caught the air. She twisted them up just enough to get some lift and soared higher into the sky. As she reached the top of the tower, Xuè Lóng came into view. He was flying the other way for the moment. She guessed he was about to turn back, so she aimed for a round building in between them with a single spire rising from the center. As she flew, she saw the dragon drifting to the left. She sped up as best she could, trying to correctly time when their paths would intersect.

She had the sun at her back, which would make spotting her more difficult. She extended her claws as she approached the round building. The dragon was coming around wide and a little faster than she had anticipated. He soared past her and she poured on the speed. She flew over his left wing and up along his body, less than two feet above his scaly skin. As she reached his head, she swiped her claws towards his face. They scraped across his eye lids and down his nose before she was forced to pull up.

The dragon twisted in mid-air and grabbed at Vampirella, his claws barely missing her. She moved just out of reach while he hovered to get his bearings. Her claws had scarred his scales. There was some blood, but he could still see. And he was pissed. She saw him look her way and then fly quickly in her direction. This was what she wanted.

Vampirella turned and flew north once more. She didn't try losing him in the buildings now. She wanted him to follow. She gained altitude as she flew. He was right behind her, his larger wings letting him cut the distance between them quickly. He was gaining ground fast when she saw Victoria Harbour in the distance. She pushed harder, climbed higher as Xuè Lóng got within a few dozen feet.

"I'm going to kill you," the dragon boomed, "then I will follow the smell of her blood and take her life, too."

Vampirella didn't respond. Instead she dove straight down just as the creature reached out for her. She plummeted over four hundred feet towards the ground. Xuè Lóng followed without hesitation. As she got close to the ground, she angled out a little, allowing her momentum to carry her over the harbor where she slammed into the water. The dragon dove right in after her.

She swam towards the south side of the harbor. She stayed as deep as she could until she got near the convention center where she shot back up towards the surface. She timed her ascension to put her right next to a helipad she'd seen earlier. She flew up out of the water, just missing the concrete extension that jutted out over the water. The larger dragon was unaware of the obstacle and slammed into it. He hit with enough force to break a large chunk of the helipad off. The impact was enough to stun him for a moment.

Vampirella raced back to where she'd left Jincan. The woman was still unconscious where she had been left. The pressure from her belt had slowed the bleeding some, but not a lot. And Xuè Lóng said he could smell her blood. Vampirella remembered her taking a healing potion of some kind after the fight with Horse-Face. She dug through the pouches until she found one that looked the same then poured it into Jincan's mouth. She then scooped the woman up into her arms and carried her inside the building.

They took the elevator to the first floor where Vampirella had planned on finding a vehicle to take them back to Zhang's, but a sign for a gym in the building across the street gave her an idea. She carried Jincan across the street and into the gym where a young man met them with a smile until he saw her condition.

His expression became serious. "I'll call for help."

"No." Vampirella grabbed him by the collar. "Take us to the locker room."

He struggled for a second before her gaze won him over. "Of course. Right this way."

He led them through the gym to the locker room. A few people looked up from their workouts but didn't seem to really care. Once inside, she told the employee to go get them some sweats. She then took Jincan into the shower. She removed the belt where she saw that her wound had stopped bleeding. It looked a day or two old at that point. She tossed the belt aside and tore off the woman's dress. She cranked on one of the showers and held Jincan up to the water, washing away all of the blood.

The employee returned with two sets of sweats and a couple of towels. "If you need anything else, I'll be at the front desk. We have a really good promotion going on right now if you want to sign up. The first six months are half off."

Vampirella ignored the man and started drying Jincan off. She then toweled herself off and got them both dressed. Both sets of sweats were dark blue and emblazoned with the gym's logo on the chest and leg. She was about to pick Jincan up again when the woman started to stir.

"Wait." She strained to open her eyes. "Please bring my belt."

Vampirella checked to see if all the blood had been rinsed off of it then tucked it under her arm. Jincan was struggling to stand. The vampire wrapped one arm around the woman and helped her out to the front desk.

"Are you two interested in becoming members?" the man asked cheerfully.

"We'll think about it." Vampirella let Jincan lean against her. "Can you call us a taxi?"

The man called a taxi and a few minutes later Vampirella was helping Jincan into the back seat where she almost immediately passed out again. Vampirella slid in and gave the driver the address of Shanghaied.

"Your friend okay?" The driver looked concerned.

"Too much time chasing the dragon."

Vampirella watched the skies the entire drive, but nothing happened. They got to the bar and she carried Jincan inside. Zhang met them at the door and led them up to his room. It was a studio set up with a small kitchenette, a bed and a couch with a TV in front of it.

"Put her on the bed." He grabbed the belt from under Vampirella's arm. "And tell me what happened."

She explained about the battle in the lobby and how they got to the roof too late to stop the ritual. He took great interest in the effect Jincan's blood had on Xuè Lóng. All the while he was going through the pouches on the cincher belt. With everything laid out on the counter, he looked concerned.

"There's stuff missing." He checked through all the vials again. "She always carries multiple health drafts and enough to make more."

"I gave her one." Vampirella checked the pouches herself. "But the belt got cut off of her. Things could've fallen out."

He looked over at Jincan. "The one potion wasn't enough. I need to make more. I need to find her supplies."

"Would this help?" She held up a hotel key.

He took the key and looked it over. "That's the Peninsula Hotel. She must have a room there. I'll head over and get what I need."

Zhang pulled the BMW into the back lot at the hotel and entered through employee entrance. He had made a call to a friend who worked at the Peninsula who would get him to the room through the service elevator. He had no idea if Xuè Lóng knew where Jincan was staying, but he wasn't going to take any chances. His friend put him on the elevator and then left. Zhang didn't want to put anyone else at risk if he could help it.

The hallway to her room was empty, but that didn't mean anything. He moved along as quietly as he could until he was a few feet from the door. He stopped and listened. There was no movement. He was about to continue on in when he heard a car door close. They were high enough that the only way he would be able to hear sounds from the street was if the window was open. Jincan never left her window open.

He reached into his coat and pulled out three wooden shuriken and held them in one hand while he gently slipped the key into the lock with the other. He let himself in quietly and looked around the room. It was a suite, and a nice one. The door opened into a sitting area with two nice chairs, a couch and a television. There was also a wet bar. There were doors into another room that had to be the bedroom. Zhang noticed two things, the window was wide open and the place was nicer than his apartment above the bar.

He moved into the suite as silently as he could. There was no sign of anything being out of place other than the open window. But the bedroom door being closed seemed odd. He crossed over and tried the handle. It was unlocked. He opened it slowly then stopped. He turned quickly and threw one of the wooden throwing stars towards the window. There was a Jiangshi there about to leap at him. The piece of wood sailed perfectly through the air and hit the creature in the forehead. It glanced at the object embedded in its skull curiously. Then the skin around it burst into flames. It spread quickly, engulfing the Jiangshi who seemed to be uncertain how to put it out. Zhang ran across the room and kicked it in the chest, sending it back out the window.

Zhang looked out and down. The body was fully ablaze and crumbling at the same time. It had all but vanished into smoke and dust before it hit the ground. Zhang looked at the remaining two shuriken. "Wood from a peach tree definitely works."

Before heading back to the bedroom, he noticed a two-foot by three-foot framed mirror on the wall by the entrance. He grabbed it and hooked his hand around the wire frame, turning it into a makeshift shield. He went back to the door to the bedroom and opened it slowly. Another Jiangshi came hopping towards him from the bathroom. He put the mirror up and the creature stopped in its tracks, starring at where his reflection should've been. Zhang had the two remaining shuriken tucked between his fingers, points forward as he made a fist. He kept the mirror up as he approached the second creature. When he got close enough, he punched it, the points of the wooden stars plunging into the Jiangshi's cheek. It's skin flamed up instantly.

He jerked his hand back and pressed the wooden weapons against his pant leg to knock out any fire on them. He didn't want to lose any more of them. He continued towards the creature, holding the mirror between them and pushing it back towards the bathroom. He drove the thing into the bathtub where the fire grew, and it turned to ash. He did a quick check of the room to see if there were any more. It was empty. Once the Jiangshi was all but destroyed, he turned the shower on to rinse away any evidence.

Then Zhang went to work. He checked every drawer, cleared out the closet, found the metal case under the bed. He checked her things and saw there was enough of what he would need to make a few healing potions. He packed up everything that was Jincan's and then checked every drawer a second time. He closed the window and locked it. He grabbed the stuff and was about to leave, stopped at the mini bar, found a small bottle of whisky that he dropped into his pocket, then headed back to the service elevator. On the first floor he found his friend, gave him the key, the bottle as a thank you and told him that they might want to wait a couple days before putting anyone else in that room... just in case.

He quickly got back to the BMW and shoved everything into the back seat.. That would get her back on her feet. But as he drove through the city, one question popped into his head that he hadn't thought to ask before. What had happened to the Soul Eater sword? Had Xuè Lóng gotten it? What could the Blood Dragon do with a blade that held the souls of some of the evilest people in China's history? The thought was mind-blowing, but he had to put that aside and get back to the bar. Jincan needed him and he wasn't going to let her down. Not again.

CHAPTER FOURTEEN

Vampirella stood in the corner, keeping an eye on the unconscious Jincan. She was still concerned that the dragon could track the woman by the scent of her blood, and she wanted to be ready. She'd removed the borrowed sweats and put them in the room she was staying in. The setup above the bar was interesting. There was the studio apartment that Zhang had and her room. There was one other room, but that door was locked. That wouldn't have stopped her if she had really wanted in, but she didn't want to disrespect her host's privacy. The whole thing was sparsely furnished, as if he was scraping by. But his car was expensive. She wondered what this said about Zhang.

She also noticed there were no windows in either room, and there had only been the one downstairs. The building would be surprisingly difficult to attack, forcing anyone coming in through a chokepoint. But if they got in, then there would be no escape for those inside. Was this a planned design or a coincidence? She didn't know enough about Zhang to make a guess.

There was a noise downstairs followed by footsteps. She tensed for a moment, then relaxed when she picked up the familiar scent. A moment later she heard Zhang coming up the stairs. She opened the door to let him in and stepped aside as he carried what she guessed was Jincan's gear. He tossed a duffle bag into the corner and then put a case up on the counter. He opened it and immediately started working.

"I haven't mixed one of these in a few years." He was measuring out a greenish-gray powder into a cup. "At least she's not watching over my shoulder. That always made me nervous."

Vampirella moved closer to watch. "I don't understand. Why didn't the one I gave her heal her completely?"

"The potions are a combination of ingredients that temporarily boost the healing factor in the human body and strengthen the immune system." He dropped a few weeds into a mortar and pestle and began grinding. "Her wound was far more serious, and the potion could only do so much. There is also the possibility of internal bleeding. A second potion would help the process along"

She took a look at some of the vials in the case. "Is this how she's lived so long?"

"That I don't know." He dumped the ground weeds into the mix. "She didn't get around to showing me everything. There were areas of her past that she was very guarded about."

He continued working, added another half-dozen items to the mix. Some were powders, others liquids.

None of it was labeled, so Vampirella couldn't really tell what the ingredients were. "Why keep this a secret? How many lives could you save if you gave this recipe to the local hospital?"

"It was once common knowledge." He shook the mixture in a single vial. "And like anything powerful, it got abused. Now the ingredients are mostly rare, coming from plants and animals that are dangerously close to extinction. If this got out, there would be a fight over what is left. It would lead to unrest, maybe even war. It's likely more would die than the sparse resources could cure. She only uses it in an effort to stop evil and save lives. And she uses it as sparingly as possible."

It was a good answer. And she got the impression it was an answer that Zhang had heard when he asked the very same question of Jincan. The bartender had finished mixing the potion and took it over to the unconscious woman. He held up her head and poured it slowly into her mouth. He then gently laid her back down.

"Now we wait." He dropped the vial back in the case then headed for the door. "I'll be right back."

He left the room and went to the locked door. He used a key and went inside, returning a few minutes later carrying a syringe. He took it to Jincan and proceeded to draw some blood. Vampirella was curious but waited to see what was going to happen. Zhang headed back to the other room. He left the door open, so she followed him. When she looked inside, she saw a very different room from the others in the building. The most obvious difference was the wall of guns and assorted weapons. Revolvers, automatics, shotguns and rifles were hung across the far wall, each with a shelf full of ammo underneath. There was even a 1930s era Tommy Gun with six drum magazines. There were also swords, pole arms, spears, shurikens, sais, and just about any other form of martial weapon she could think of. Next to the arsenal were metal shelves filled with body armor, then food and water supplies. It resembled a war bunker.

The other side of the room, on the other hand, was like a crime lab filled with computers and equipment that looked like the stuff on television police dramas. Zhang was over in that corner putting a drop of Jincan's blood onto a slide.

She moved into the room. "What are you doing?"

"You said her blood burned Xuè Lóng when it touched him." He put the slide under a magnifying glass. "If I can figure out why, then it might let me figure out a way to kill him."

He began to work and moved about the equipment like he knew what he was doing. Vampirella took a seat on a stool near a work bench and watched him. "What are you?"

He looked up. "What do you mean?"

"The other night I got the impression you were a bartender with a knowledge of the supernatural world." She gestured to the room around her. "Yet here you are with an armory and lab. You obviously have a history with Jincan and can mix the same potions she uses. You've dived head first into this situation with Xuè Lóng and have been helping us without any reservations. I know about the ghost you dealt with in the past. But this looks like someone who's gone to war."

He put his head down and sighed. "I signed up for the war, went through all the training and then went AWOL the moment things got real."

"This doesn't look like AWOL," she said.

"When I was younger, I wanted to find answers and started digging into every rumor I could find." He continued to work while he talked. "It eventually led me to Jincan. She was going after a particularly evil spirit that was haunting an orphanage. It was terrorizing the children but avoided being seen by the employees. They thought the kids were making it up. Then one of the orphans, a fourteen-year-old girl, committed suicide. She jumped off the fifth-floor roof. The note she left behind had a detailed account of everything she had suffered. They tried to cover it up, but one of the other kids stole the note and snuck it out to a reporter.

"When the story hit the news, it was the talk of the city for a few days. I heard about it and one night I decided to sneak in and see what I could find. It happened to be the same night Jincan had decided to do the same thing. She caught me sneaking through the place. I had the sharp edge of her sword against my throat. She demanded to know who I was. I explained I was sickened by the news report and wanted to help. She said I looked sincere and told me to follow her. I watched as she tracked down the spirit and banished it. Before she could leave, I begged her to train me. To teach me to do the things she could. She said no and vanished.

"I was disappointed but I wasn't discouraged. I went to college with what I'm told was the oddest duel major ever, criminology and mythological studies. I wanted to understand the supernatural and use science to find answers. My professors all thought I was crazy, but I was a straight 'A' student, so they left me alone. A year or so after college I was out investigating a series of strange disappearances. Seven people had gone missing near the harbor over a two-year period. The victims were different ages, different genders and different races. The abductions were so random the authorities hadn't figured out they were connected. I figured out it was a spirit possessing various people to do the abducting. I went to confront the person being possessed at the time, but Jincan was already there. She forced the spirit out of the guy's body and banished it.

"I was despondent. All my hard work and she beat me to him. I went home to sulk, but she was waiting for me there. She'd been keeping an eye on me all those years and explained that I had led her to the spirit, and she was extremely impressed. She said I was ready to be trained. Over the next couple of years, she trained me in potions, magic and martial arts. It was a hundred times more intense than university and I learned so much. But it was all learning, practicing and training. When it came time to confront a ghost, she did that. I was just there for support. I carried the backup potions. I got tired of it.

"The next time we had a situation, a spirit haunting a library, I did the research and figured out who the spirit was and where he had died. But I told Jincan a lie. I wanted a chance to use all the stuff I had learned. I went to the site, I summoned the ghost forth and when I was face-to-face with it, I froze. I couldn't think. I couldn't move. But before he could attack me, Jincan appeared and took care of him. She knew I was lying to her, followed me and saved my life. She acted like she'd expected me to do it all along.

"I was ashamed. I was a coward and I couldn't look her in the eyes." He finally looked up at Vampriella. "I left. Tried to walk away from it all, but I couldn't. I knew there were horrible things out there, and I couldn't pretend otherwise. I kept my ear to the ground. Opened up this bar and then overcompensated by using my money to buy weapons and equipment even though I believed I would never use them."

Vampirella picked up one of the wooden shurikens. "Yet tonight you raced over to Jincan's hotel and without a second thought took out two Jiangshi so you could retrieve the things you needed to save her life. Unless I've lost something in translation, that doesn't sound like a coward to me."

He stopped and turned toward the vampire. "I hadn't really thought about it."

"You were more concerned about her than yourself." She smiled. "I believe that falls more into the heroic category. These creatures can be terrifying. Xuè Lóng is an actual dragon. The Jiangshi are the undead. You're supposed to be scared of these things. And when you faced one on your own, you had doubts that made you freeze. But when someone else's life was on the line, you did what had to be done. You're not a coward, you're human."

Zhang stood quietly for a few minutes. She watched as his mouth slowly turned up into a smile. He looked like he was about to speak when a machine behind him beeped. He turned and pulled a printout off and read it over. "This is amazing."

She got up and walked over to look at the paper. "What is it?

"There are elements in her blood that just don't make sense." He showed her the results. "I'm not even sure you could call it blood. It's also toxic."

"What do you mean?" She couldn't make sense of the printout.

"You're a vampire. You drink blood." He held up the rest of the sample he took. "Does this smell like normal blood to you?"

She'd dealt with cleaning it up earlier but had been too preoccupied to pay attention to the smell. She held the glass vial up to her nose and winced. "Definitely not."

"I don't know what would happen if you drank it. But I don't recommend it." He took the vial back. "But from the toxicology I can tell you that it would definitely be poisonous for me to drink. I can't say exactly which poison, but this blood would be lethal to humans."

"How is that even possible?" She couldn't get the pungent smell out of her nostrils. "If it's poisonous to humans, how is she still alive?"

"That is another excellent question." He grabbed a pad and started writing down some notes. "But since we're dealing with a woman who is over six hundred years old, it's safe to say the rule book was thrown out a long time ago."

"It seems odd that a mythical dragon of immense power would be affected by something poisonous." Vampirella picked up the vial and looked at the blood. "Xuè Lóng talked about following the scent of her blood, but this doesn't smell like blood."

"There is still blood there, it just happens to be mixed with some kind of poison." He made some more notes. "Maybe he can tell the difference and pick out the traces of her blood because he's using her brother's body. Their blood would be similar."

"I don't know." She leaned back against the work bench. "He controlled the blood the same way he controlled the blood of the cultists. If there was something that different about it, you'd think he would've noticed. Unless he can't sense the poison."

He turned to look at her. "I'm all for figuring out the why, but let's put that for later. Right now my concern is how do we use this against him. Her blood was the only thing to cause him pain."

"I don't know, the helipad probably gave him a bit of a headache." She punched her fist up into her open palm making a smacking sound. "It definitely stunned him."

"I don't think I can weaponize helipads." He took the vial back from her. "The blood I may be able to work with."

"If you are able to come up with something," Vampirella asked, "how will you know if it will work?"

"I don't know." He looked around the room. "Not sure how I could test it. Would've been nice if you'd gotten a piece of scale or something when you fought him."

A voice came from the doorway. "You mean like this?"

Vampirella and Zhang turned to see Jincan leaning against the door jam. She looked pale and weak. There was sweat on her forehead and she held one hand against her wounded stomach. But in the other hand she held up part of a red dragon scale. The piece was about the size of a quarter with jagged edges. "This was stuck in my belt. By the way, where are my dress and sword?"

"The dress I can explain." Vampirella walked over to her. "I didn't see the sword when you went flying off the building."

"I'd really like to get it back." Jincan finished the sentence and began to collapse.

Vampirella caught her and carried her back to the bed and laid her down again. Zhang checked her wound. The scab was coming off and it looked like it was going to leave a scar. He seemed pleased with her progress. “She needs some more rest, but I think she’s going to be okay.”

“Okay then.” Vampirella walked over to the stairs. “You keep an eye on her. I’m going to go look for her sword.”

CHAPTER FIFTEEN

Vampirella returned to the lobby of the Nina Tower and found it to be functioning as if it was any other day. Someone has removed the glass from the orbs and the axe was gone. There was a cleaning crew doing the floors. She figured they were called for the excess dust left over from the Jiangshi fight. She was dressed in street clothes she'd grabbed from Zhang's seemingly endless supply and walked in causally. She smiled at the security guard and made her way to the elevators. No one tried to stop her. She took the first elevator up to the fortieth floor, then switched to the second and made her way to the top. A few minutes later she was walking out onto the roof.

The roof was empty and again, there was no sign of any disturbance. The cultist bodies were gone. The Jiangshi were gone. No sign of the Blood Dragon. Had she not been there, she'd have no idea that anything had happened just a few hours before. She walked around the perimeter of the roof, looking for anything out of place. She hadn't really paid attention when she'd come up there before. The circle of undead and the flying blood were a bit distracting.

The ritual had taken place on a large area that looked to double as a dance floor for parties. There was also a bar, and around the edges there were a variety of types of seating. Some were individual chairs while others were couches. There were tables and a few of those outdoor heaters. It would be a nice place to hang out after work if she had a normal job.

She walked over to where she'd seen Jincan get clawed by Xuè Lóng. She stood where she thought the spot was and started looking around the area. Over to her right was a couch, table and two chairs. They were far enough away from the center that they hadn't been touched by the cultists. She saw that there was something under the couch. She walked over and squatted down to take a closer look. She saw what she believed was the handle to a sword. With one hand she lifted the couch up over her head and grabbed the sword with the other. To her amazement, it was the Soul Eater. Somehow in all the confusion, not one had noticed it slide under the couch. She put the couch back in its place then stood.

It seemed too easy to her. She turned around expecting trouble and noticed that someone was standing there. It was an older man with a lit cigarette in his mouth, except the cigarette was barely hanging in place. The man's mouth was agape and his eyes wide. She figured he must have seen her lifting the couch. She walked towards him, trying to make eye contact.

"You didn't see what you thought you saw," she said in a calm voice.

He responded in Cantonese. Vampirella could recognize the language but didn't know enough to give the guy any real hypnotic suggestions. But she did know one phrase. "Fan gauu."

The man's eyes shut immediately, his knees buckled and he would've fallen to the ground had Vampirella not caught him. She scooped him up into her arms. His cigarette dropped and she smushed it out with her boot. She then placed him gently on the nearest couch in the shade. He'd have some questions when he woke up, but she had no intention of being around to answer them. She slipped off his jacket and wrapped it around the sword. She wasn't sure if Xuè Lóng had anyone watching the building, but she didn't want to draw attention to herself either way.

She took the two elevators back down to the ground floor, then waited for the security guard to be busy with someone else before heading for the front door. Once outside, she flagged down a taxi and headed back to Shanghaied. As she sat in the back with the concealed sword in her lap, she hoped that finding it meant their luck was changing. They seemed to be one step behind on everything and the Blood Dragon was already back on Earth. They could use things to start going their way if they were going to stop whatever he had planned next.

Hua got up again. She still felt weak, but better than she had. She heard noise from the other room and followed the sound. She found Zhang working on a computer in his armory/lab. He was so focused he didn't hear her enter. It gave her a chance to look at him closely. She hadn't seen him in quite a while. The graying temples were new as were some wrinkles around the eyes. She wondered how long it had been. More than ten years, at least. Maybe twenty. She'd lived so long that decades passed like they were nothing. She remembered helping one man and then going back to the same family later to discover his grandchildren had grandchildren. It was one of the reasons she didn't get close to anyone. She didn't want to watch anyone else she loved die.

Zhang was different, though. When she first met him, he was young and determined, the kind of person that would just end up getting themselves killed. Even though she wanted nothing to do with that, she kept an eye on him over the years. When it became clear that he could be a useful asset and was smart enough to stay out of trouble, she decided to train him. She kept him away from danger as long as she could, but she knew one day he would have to jump into the fray. She hoped his tendency to freeze up under duress would make him focus on supporting her cause but keep him out of harm's way. She never quite understood why he left. Why he tossed away all the work he'd put in and decided to open a bar. Maybe she'd never understand it.

"What are you doing?" she asked, trying not to startle him.

He turned. "Oh, I didn't know you were up. Are you feeling better?"

"Quite a bit, thank you." She pointed at the computer. "What are you working on?"

"Vampirella explained how your blood affected the dragon." He turned the screen so she could see it. "I've been analyzing it, trying to figure out why and how we might use that to our advantage. But your blood is far from normal. I'm having a hard time figuring out what exactly it is."

"That's a long story." She shifted nervously.

He turned to face her. "Long or not, figuring it out could make the difference in beating Xuè Lóng."

She didn't like talking about her past. Any of it. There were no happy memories to share, but what he would need to know were some of the worst after her parents' death. She didn't relish the idea of going through it. But, as dramatic as it sounded, the fate of the world was on the line.

She took a seat next to him. "You know about my brother and the woman who started teaching me about potions. But there was another..."

Hua had been studying for years and was becoming frustrated. It had been almost a decade since her brother became Jiangshi and she had no idea where to find him. She thought she was getting close two years prior when she had tracked down a couple of creatures like him. She was able to deal with them, but after that there was no trace of more. She dove into her training and studies, quickly surpassing her instructors and moving on to the ones that trained them. Where it hadn't been hard to locate new instructors early on, she was struggling to find new things to learn. Her last mentor spoke of someone he had studied with, a man known only as the Teacher. He was said to live on Mount Emei, thousands of feet up in an area nearly impossible to get to. But Hua was determined.

It took her months to travel to the base of the mountain and two weeks to climb to the spot she was told to look for. The face of the mountain jutted out in nearly a sheer climb, one that most would avoid. She'd been told to climb up the face and look for a crevice no bigger than a single person. She passed it twice before finding the spot. She squeezed into the crevice that went back maybe ten feet. Once she was in all the way, she saw a crawl space at the base of the crevice that she could just slide into. She crawled on her hands and knees in the dark for a few minutes before seeing a bit of light at the end of the tunnel.

When she got there, she squeezed up and out into a circular valley that she could walk across in under a minute. The walls of the valley went up a long way and grew closer together near the top, creating a crown that still allowed the sunlight in. It would be almost impossible to find the place by accident. In the center of the valley was a tiny hut that looked to be made from the two trees that grew there. There was a man standing in front of the hut with his arms folded in front of him.

"How long did you plan to keep me waiting?" he asked.

"Excuse me?" Hua approached cautiously. "I'm not sure how you think..."

"You're hoping to be my new student. But you could barely find the entrance. Not a good way to start." He pointed to three various sized jars next to him. "They don't like to be kept waiting either. Shall we begin?"

She looked at the man in disbelief. How could he have known she was coming? The only one who knew was her instructor who gave her the location and there was no way he could've gotten a message here before her. The Teacher was a tall, thin man with short, dark hair and a beard. She wasn't certain he was Chinese as his look was rather unique, unlike anyone she'd seen before. His clothes were unusual for the time but would best be described as makeshift jeans and a poncho. It was cold in the mountain, but he seemed unaffected by it. His expression betrayed nothing. He just stood there, waiting for her to do something.

She walked over to the three jars and lifted one of the lids slowly. Inside was a white-lipped pit viper that hissed at her and looked ready to strike. She slammed the lid back down. She looked up at the man who simply nodded and motioned to the second, slightly smaller jar. She lifted the lid and found a scorpion inside. She replaced the lid and looked to the smallest jar. It would have fit into the palm of her hand. She lifted the lid and found a golden colored silkworm. It seemed out of place with the other two. She closed the lid and looked at the Teacher.

"The problem with most instructors is they spend years teaching the mundane." He pulled out a piece of wax and walked over to one of the trees. "Students get bored and lose interest or the instructors spend years working with students that aren't worth teaching. I'm going to teach you the deadliest thing I know first. If you survive, then you're worth my time and effort. If that doesn't work for you, you can leave now."

He picked up a twig from the ground then walked back towards her. Hua was tired from her journey. She expected to have to implore the teacher to train her. Explain her story and why she was worthy. That's how it was with almost all of the other instructors. Maybe if she wasn't exhausted, she would've questioned what was happening, asked how it was dangerous. Instead she just nodded.

"Good." The Teacher pointed to the jars. "Put the silkworm and the scorpion in with the viper."

She looked at the three jars. She knew the scorpion and snake were dangerous and really didn't want to be bitten. She looked at the jars and realized that they were quite a bit different in size. She didn't want to have the lid off too long for fear of them getting out or attacking. She lifted the lid of the scorpion's jar and dropped the smaller jar inside. She then closed the lid and moved over to the viper's jar where she dropped the two smaller jars inside.

The Teacher didn't say a word. He shook the twig and the end caught on fire. He held it to the end of the wax stick until is was melting. He handed the stick to Hua. "Seal the jar with this."

She ran the wax along the lip of the jar until she had a solid coating all around. She then took a step back to let it cool. She handed the wax back to him and he blew on it. The melted part solidified immediately, and he tucked it back in his pocket.

"What we are doing is called Gu." He sat down on the ground a few feet from the jar. "The making of poison. This particular poison is called Jincan, after the golden silkworm that is part of it. Depending on the dose, it can be used for everything from manipulating a loved one to causing illness and even death. It has another purpose, but I'll tell you of that later. For now, we wait."

"That's it?" She sat down next to him. "We put them in a jar together and wait?"

"Oh, I forgot a crucial step." He reached over, picked up the jar and shook the hell out of it before placing it back on the ground. "Now we wait."

They sat for hours in silence, watching the unmoving jars. Hua found it annoying at first. She'd traveled all that distance to watch a jar? She wondered if she'd found the wrong obscure crevice on the side of the mountain. Could there be two and this guy was insane? That actually sounded more absurd than what she was doing. She continued to sit there, and while she sat, she found herself relaxing. The constant anger that boiled inside of her eased up. She realized how peaceful the little valley was. How the crease of sunlight that came in from above felt good on her face. Even the cold wasn't bothering her.

"Most don't know that the Jincan is one of the deadliest creatures on the planet." He spoke so softly she hadn't realized he'd started talking at first. "The venom from any of those three can kill. But you place them in a container together and force them to fight, they bite each other, causing the venom to pool together in the survivor. Then you extract that venom."

She turned to look at him. "That makes no sense at all."

"Don't mess with the magic." He got to his feet. "It should be ready."

He handed her a knife and she cut open the wax seal. When she opened the lid, she found only the viper was still alive, but it wasn't moving. The venom from the scorpion and the silkworm was killing it. The teacher handed her a small wooden bowl then he grabbed the snake and put its mouth over the lip of the bowl. He squeezed the side of the viper's head and the venom started dripping out. When he stopped, the snake had passed. And he placed it back in the jar with the others.

"Now the most important part." He handed her the bowl. "Take a sip."

Hua was stunned. The Teacher had just explained how deadly this venom was and how it could kill. And he was asking her to drink it. She felt like tossing it to the ground and leaving. But she didn't. Something told her to trust this man. He told her to take a sip of the poison, so she did just that. She held the bowl to her mouth and felt the liquid pour over her lips and hit her tongue. It burned a little as she swallowed it. She looked back at the bowl and saw she'd taken only a small amount. She showed it to the teacher.

"Very good." He took the bowl. "Your stomach will hurt tonight and you won't be able to sleep. It will pass. Then next time you'll drink a little more and it will be the same. Eventually you'll be able to drink an entire bowl full and it will not affect you."

She bowed her head. "Is that why you had me drink it? To build up an immunity?"

"Yes." He started to go inside the hut then looked back. "That and it will stop you from aging."

Jincan finished her story and looked at Zhang. He looked shocked. She hadn't thought about the Teacher in a long time. His lessons shaped her. Made her the warrior she was. But they were always dangerous. She could've easily died thousands of times with him.

"Does that tell you what you need?" she asked.

"It gives me a better idea of what I'm looking at." Zhang looked concerned. "Where you ever going to teach that lesson to me?"

She thought about it for a moment. "No. I wouldn't do that to you."

CHAPTER SIXTEEN

Vampirella returned to Shanghaied and found Zhang and Jincan sitting in the armory. She thought she might be interrupting a moment, but at this point she didn't really care. She walked in without saying a word and put the sword down on the bench.

Jincan grabbed Soul Eater and checked it over. "How did you get it back?"

"It was simple." She walked over to the weapon wall. "It had slid under a couch."

"That's lucky," Zhang said.

"Probably not." Vampirella picked the Tommy gun off the wall and looked at it. "It might have slid across the roof unnoticed and tucked safely under a piece of furniture. But I'm guessing Xuè Lóng wanted me to find it so I could lead him back to you."

Zhang hopped to his feet. "Then why do what he wanted?"

"So we could confront him." Jincan nodded her approval to her friend. "How else were we going to find him? Now he may come to us."

Vampirella put the gun back. "I hope you have the blood thing figured out. We're probably going to need it very soon."

"I think I do." He grabbed his papers to show her. "The blood contains an amazingly high amount of..."

She held her hand up. "I don't need the details. I just need to know how long until it will be ready."

"I haven't had a chance to test it yet." He held up the cultist knife Vampirella had brought him. "I've covered this with an extract of Jincan's blood. It should be toxic to just about anything, but I think it's especially potent to Xuè Lóng because of the shared DNA between Hua and Fan."

Vampirella took the blade. "Stab him with this? That's the plan?"

"Pretty much." He pointed to a glass full of blood. "If I have some time, I'll try to coat a few more things so the knife isn't our only weapon. If you're going to use it, try to make it someplace that will count. The closer to a vital organ the better."

She cautiously slid the dagger into her boot. "Gotcha."

The conversation was interrupted by a loud thud above them. All three looked towards the ceiling, realizing they were out of time.

Vampirella turned to Jincan. "Are you ready to fight?"

"I could use a few minutes to put together a potion or two." Jincan clenched her blade tight.

"I'll see if I can buy you some time." Vampirella tore off her t-shirt. "But don't take too long."

The vampire tore off the pants as well, leaving only her red sling suit and black knee-high boots. She'd done enough running and escaping on this trip. She was going to confront the evil creature as she was more inclined to do. She thought about going up to the roof but decided against it. She wanted to take away any advantage the Blood Dragon might have. He'd have more room to move up there. On the ground, between the parked cars and lamp posts, she might be able to outmaneuver him. Assuming she could get him to come down to ground level.

She walked out the front door and onto the street. It was the middle of the afternoon and the street was filled with people. She didn't like fighting in the daytime. Too many people, not enough shadows. She wasn't being given a choice. As she exited the bar, she saw that cars had come to a stop, people were frozen in place, gawking up at the creature on the roof. It was as if they'd never seen a dragon before.

She reached the middle of the street, turned and looked up. "Can I help you?"

"Yes. I've come for my sister." There was an odd refinement to the dragon's raspy voice. "Fetch her for me and I will let you live."

"I'm sorry to be the one to tell you, she's dead." Vampirella raised her voice to just short of a shout. "You gutted her and she passed before I got her back here."

He growled out a breath. "You know I can smell her blood."

"Yeah. It got all over the place." She points at the door. "I was just starting to clean up when I heard you land. If you don't mind, I need to get back to it. It's making a mess of the floors."

"You're not nearly as clever as you think you are," he spit out.

"I don't know. I do pretty well." She shrugged. "Though I probably should've thought twice before picking my outfit. The guy behind me is ignoring you and keeps staring at my ass."

One of the pedestrians behind her turned beet read and quickly started looking up at the dragon.

Xuè Lóng shouted down. "Why are you wasting my time?!"

"You've been waiting thousands of years to come back to Earth and destroy it." She gestured to the things around her. "I live here. I'm going to do whatever I can to stop you from succeeding."

"And you think antagonizing me is going to help?" He shook his head. "You are but an insignificant worm. I will kill you and then go for my sister."

She motioned towards the ground. "Come on down and give it a shot. If you think you can beat me."

He responded by flapping his wings and soaring up into the air, then banking around towards her. Vampirella looked around and saw all the people still watching. "Run, you idiots!"

The dragon swooped down on top of a Volvo wagon. The driver dove out of the vehicle just as the creature crushed it beneath its feet. This was finally enough of a sign to the crowd for them to turn and flee in terror. Vampirella took a step back and prepared to fight. She realized that Xuè Lóng had gotten bigger between the roof and the ground. His wings, which had looked to span about twenty feet before were easily thirty feet across. His head alone was now as big as her and his mouth looked as if it could swallow her in one gulp. If his intent was to intimidate, he was doing a good job of it.

She whispered to herself, "I hope I bought them enough time."

The dragon lunged at her, biting at her head. She ducked under the attack. She punched up into his exposed throat. It felt like she had just hit a brick wall. Xuè Lóng didn't seem to even notice the strike. He swung at her with his left claw. She rolled forward to get out of the way and let her momentum carry her onto the front of the crushed car, then she kicked up with both feet. Her boots slammed into his chest and again he didn't react. He jumped off the car and swung at her with his tail as he passed over. It hit her in the side, throwing her across the street. She landed, rolled and slammed into the front door of the bar.

She checked to make sure dagger was still in her boot. It was. She got back to her feet and watched the dragon attempting to turn. It had to tuck its wings in against its body and it still moved a few cars out of the way while doing it. Being bigger meant he was slower. She looked him over from tail to snout, trying to find a weak spot. His scales were just too thick. His eyes were a possible target as was the inside of his mouth. The scales around his joints seemed to be a little smaller.

The dragon moved towards her. She extended her claws and dashed as fast as she could at him. When she got close enough, she jumped and reached her hands forward. Her claws racked across his eye lids. He wasn't fast enough to block her, but he did get his eyes closed just in time. His head spun around quicker than she'd expected. His teeth sliced across her leg as she tried to avoid the attack. She swung, her claws racking across the top of his open mouth. She smelled the blood that started to flow from the wound. He pulled away as she leapt to the side. She thought she was clear, but then his tail hit her in the back. She went flying again, this time through the bar's glass window.

Shards flew everywhere as she crashed into one of the tables. She scrambled to her feet. "I really hate that tail."

"Are you okay?" Zhang's voice called down from the top of the stairs.

"Yeah." She shook the glass out of her hair. "Feel free to join in at any time."

She crossed the bar and went out the door. On the other side, Xuè Lóng held a woman in his claw. Vampirella guessed she'd been too scared to run. Before the vampire could react, the dragon bit the woman's head off and spit it through the broken bar window. He drained the blood from her body like a kid sucking the sugar from a pixy stix. As he drank deeply, he grew again. He ended up being as tall as a two-story building and his wings were twice that wide.

She wasn't sure why he'd chosen to grow again. He was already as hard as steel. She couldn't wait to see what his plan was. She charged him. He took a swing at her with his left claw, but she slid under it and came up just short of his back leg. She grabbed the dagger from her boot and slammed it as hard as she could down into the area between his toes. The scales seemed smaller there and she was able to just penetrate the skin. The dragon growled in pain and kicked out, hitting Vampirella in the chest. It felt like a sledgehammer and knocked her off her feet. She was barely able to hang on to the knife as she fell back to the ground.

She got up and moved as his tail swung past. She thought for a second that he didn't seem quite as big as he had just a moment before. He stood up on his hind legs and slammed both front claws into the second-floor wall of the bar. The bricks cracked and he left a good-sized indentation. He leaned back and slammed again. More damage to the wall. Vampirella figured a few more hits and he could break through. This explained why he'd grown, to bring the building down.

She waited until he was about to strike again and raced in. She sliced across his exposed armpit. He let out another painful growl as the small dagger sliced through the scales and drew blood. She kept moving and cut across the same spot on the other side. She let her speed carry her out of range and watched as Xuè Lóng shrunk down again. Not back to where he'd started, but enough that he wouldn't be able to hit the building in the same spot again.

The dragon appeared to be in a lot of pain. Vampirella decided to press her luck and dove for his head. He grabbed her out of the air and slammed her hard to the ground. The move was so quick and violent that she lost the dagger, hearing it clang off the ground as she felt herself smashed into the asphalt. He then shifted forward, putting his weight on top of her. Her body screamed in pain, her bones on the verge of snapping.

Xuè Lóng leaned down putting his enormous face close to hers. "I'm going to pulverize your bones to dust. Then I'm going to peel off your flesh and pluck out your organs and muscles like a cluster of grapes. And the fact that you're a vampire means you'll be alive to watch through most of it."

Vampirella couldn't move. She tried to reach for the dagger, but it was too far out of range. The dragon could kill her, but he seemed determined to torture her first. She hoped that Jincan and Zhang had finished and were about to come out and join the fight. Give her a chance to get up. She heard something. Someone was coming their way.

She tried to turn her head, but the noise wasn't coming from the bar. It was coming from many different directions all at once. It was the sound of really long strides. Or hops. Then she saw the first one come into view. A Jiangshi was coming up the street towards them. Then she saw two more right behind the first. She craned her head the other way and saw a half dozen more coming down towards them. A few appeared on the rooftops behind them. More on the roof of the bar and the neighboring buildings. The sounds kept going. More and more of them were arriving. Too many for her to count.

The Jiangshi formed around their master. They leaped down from the rooftops or made their way along the street until they stood in a half circle in front of the bar. She pushed against the claw holding her down, but it wouldn't budge. The dragon rolled his palm and Vampirella felt two ribs and something in her left arm snap. She fought back against the pain and focused on trying to find a way out.

"Before I get to you," The dragon snarled in her face. "I'm going to let them take care of my wayward sister. It seems fitting with how many of their kind she's killed over the years."

She spat in his face. "You're too much of a coward to fight her yourself? You're afraid of your little sister?"

He laughed. "Is that supposed to taunt me into doing something stupid? Make me want to go prove my manhood or something? You really don't know when you've lost, do you?"

He flicked his tail out and it smashed down the door. The move made him shift the tiniest amount of weight off of Vampirella and she took that moment to shove against his palm with all her might. His hand didn't budge at all. He just pushed down harder and she felt pain from too many places to keep track.

He addressed the Jiangshi. "Kill anyone inside."

"No. You can't." Vampirella could barely speak.

"Of course I can." He smiled at her. "I'm a god. I do what I want. And if you think there's any chance that Hua might be able to fend them off... there's a hundred and seventeen of them. Not my full army. These were just the ones nearby that could get here in time for the fight."

The Jiangshi silently formed up in front of them. There were so many she could no longer see the door. They would make their way in, go up the stairs and no matter how Zhang and Jincan fought back, they would eventually be overwhelmed by the sheer number of creatures. She couldn't stop them. She couldn't break free. She was powerless to do anything.

CHAPTER SEVENTEEN

Zhang's heart was racing as he finished loading the duffle bag. He didn't bother to zip it shut as he threw the strap over the top of his head. It hung across his chest with the bag dangling under his right arm. He had two Glock 17s in holsters on his hips, both had the twenty-one round magazines. He grabbed the Tommy gun from the wall.

"They're coming in!" Jincan shouted from the doorway.

He slapped the barrel mag into the machine gun and chambered the first round. "Let's do this."

Jincan stood on the landing wearing her last black and gold dress. Her belt was in place and her pouches were full. She downed one of the potions and asked, "Spirit of the Rabbit, please come aid me."

Zhang moved past her and took position at the top of the stairs. He was scared, he was about to field test a theory by attacking a swarm of the undead. He'd be insane not to be scared. Hell, he was insane for even being there. He had a secret back exit in case of emergencies, but he wasn't going to use it. He wasn't going to leave Jincan. He took a deep breath, adjusted his grip on the gun and waited.

The first Jiangshi entered the small hallway and Zhang fired. Though the gun was capable of more, he fired just one round. The pop of the gun would've been deafening if he hadn't thought to put in earplugs earlier. The shot hit its target dead square in the chest. The creature stopped and looked at the wound. Something like surprise or worry shown on its face just before it crumbled to dust.

Zhang cheered, "Yes!"

He moved down two steps at a time until he saw more of the enemy, then he opened fire in three round bursts. He tore through two more Jiangshi quickly and kept moving forward. When he got far enough down the stairs, he began sweeping side to side, his intent to clear some space for them in the bar. They'd talked about staying at the top and using the stairwell as a chokepoint, forcing the Jiangshi into the tiny space where they'd be easier to kill, but they weren't sure what was going on with Vampirella. If they could get outside, they might be able to help.

When he reached the bottom step, he took out his seventh undead and switched magazines. The creatures continued to push forward, undaunted by the fate of their friends. Jincan pushed past him, Soul Eater in hand, and confronted the nearest one. It swung at her immediately, claws going for her face. She sliced through its wrist and the hand went flying over her shoulder and hit the ground by Zhang's feet. She was swinging the sword with her right hand because her left hand carried a gift he'd given her, a small wooden stake made from a peach tree. She drove that into the Jiangshi's forehead and the creature crumbled to nothing.

She turned and smiled at him. "I like it."

He popped the action on the Tommy gun and started firing again. He blew away two, literally, as the wind gusted through the open door carrying the dust across the room. Things were slowing down for him. He watched as Jincan stepped in front of him to attack a creature. He simply shifted to the other side and found another target. A quick burst of bullets, and another was taken out of the game. This definitely wasn't something he wanted to do on a regular basis, but now he knew he could step up when he needed to. And he was finally getting a chance to fight at her side.

Another wave of Jiangshi pushed in through the door. He moved towards the far wall, which allowed him to look out the broken front window. He couldn't see anything but a wave of the undead. He did the math in his head and realized he didn't have enough bullets. Nowhere near enough.

"There's a lot of company outside." He fired through the window at the cluster of creatures. "I hope you don't have dinner plans."

Jincan was surrounded by three Jiangshi. She used the wooden dagger as a feint, then slashed across the first one's face with the sword. It interrupted the tattoo and the creature fell. She kicked the second one back while driving the dagger into the neck of the third. When the second one popped back up to attack, she took his head off with the Soul Eater.

She turned to Zhang. "Focus on the ones in front of you. We'll get through this."

He was looking out the window at the group he'd opened fire on. As he hoped, the bullets tore through the first line of bad guys and into the ones behind them. The problem was the blood he'd dipped each round in before loading must have been wiped off going through the first body. They weren't destroying the second ones hit as he theorized. No killing two for one, it seemed. He moved in and started taking single shots to conserve bullets. He focused on the door and let Jincan clean up the rest of the room.

She was moving through the bar like lightning, her sword swinging wide and her dagger plunging deep. But the number of Jiangshi was increasing even with Zhang trying to control the door. Some were jumping in through the window. As soon as she took out one, two more would appear. She stabbed at one with her dagger only to have her wrist grabbed by another. A third clawed her in the shoulder and her hand flexed open. The wooden dagger was gone. They started pushing against her, clawing at her skin. When her back hit the bar, she spun around and leaped over it.

She grabbed a bottle of vodka in her free hand. "Zhang! I think it's time for plan B!"

"I told you how much I hate that plan, right?" He clicked another barrel magazine into place knowing it was his last. "Do it!"

She hurled the bottle of vodka at one of the Jiangshi and it broke open, spilling alcohol all over it and the other undead around him. She grabbed another bottle and threw it. Then another. Each bottle pushed one of the creatures back for just a second. Enough time to grab another and throw it.

While this was happening, Zhang started working his way back towards the stairs. He had chosen this building because of its defensibility. But he also liked it for its old, wooden construction. Plan B had been around for a very long time and he was ready. He stopped at the doors to the stairs and waited. Jincan was throwing the last of the bottles at the Jiangshi. She sprinted around the bar and through the door. Zhang pulled a flare out of his bag and lit it. He tossed it into the puddle of spilt alcohol on the floor. It went up instantly as did all of the soaked undead around it. The fire spread quickly, destroying the creatures inside as more continued to enter. They had their orders.

Vampirella smelled the smoke long before she saw the flames. She was still pinned under Xuè Lóng's palm and having no luck getting free. When the flames started dancing up the side of the building more than half of the Jiangshi had gone inside. It took a few moments for the dragon to figure out what was going on.

"Stop!" he shouted. "Move away from the building!"

They backed away as the flames grew higher. Xuè Lóng watched the door like he was just waiting for his sister to burst through. It didn't happen. He shifted to the side, trying to crane his head over to see inside the window.

Vampirella felt some of the pressure lift off of her, and it was just enough. She got her arms against his hand and pushed. Xuè Lóng was already a bit off balance and this tipped him over. The big dragon crashed over onto his side. Vampirella was on her feet and moving out of range. She thought about grabbing the dagger, but it was now under him. She went the other way. She ducked behind a van and assessed her situation. There was the Blood Dragon, close to fifty Jiangshi, she'd lost the dagger with Jincan's blood on it and it looked like she was now alone in the fight.

Looking through the window of the van, she saw the dragon getting up and looking pissed. The building was engulfed in flames and the Jiangshi were surprisingly close together. Oh, and the keys to the van were in the ignition. She checked the door and it was unlocked. Someone must have been in it and decided to run instead of drive away. The van was already pointed at the dragon, so Vampirella started the engine, popped it into drive and slammed the peddle to the floor. The vehicle lurched forward and raced down the street. She leapt out of the door just as it slammed into Xuè Lóng. It sent him staggering back a few feet but didn't seem to do any real damage. The van on the other hand flipped up and over and crashed into the crowd of Jiangshi. Most moved out of the way, but a few we crushed by the half ton steel object.

This got the Blood Dragon's attention. "Get Vampirella!"

The swarm of Jiangshi sped towards her. She was ready to stand her ground when she heard a voice above her. "Mind if I join you?" She looked up and saw Zhang sliding down a rope from a building three down from his bar.

"How did you get out?" she asked.

"Roof access hatch." He hit the ground next to her. "Cut across to a rope I had stashed up there."

"What about Jincan?"

He pointed back up to the roof. "She'll be right down."

Jincan was running across the roof then dove off directly towards Xuè Lóng. She had her sword out over her head and was ready to strike. The dragon saw her at the last minute and moved out of the way. She landed on the top of a Toyota, rolled down the hood and hit the ground running. He swiped at her with his tail. She leapt over it and sliced at his back leg. She hit the spot where his tendon would be, but the scales were too thick and the blade just skidded across.

Zhang got a few more shots off with the Tommy gun before it was empty. He tossed it aside and dropped the bag, then drew his two Glocks. "Let's make this count."

Vampirella looked at him. "Just don't shoot me."

"I'll try not to." He grinned.

She ran forward and met the group of Jiangshi. The creatures were strong and fast, but not faster than she was. They were deadly, but their stiff limbs made them less agile than a normal fighter. Their attacks were wide swings with their claws or bites. She moved in close enough to negate their claw attacks and used her own claws to slice through their face tattoos before the Jiangshi could bite her. The move worked, but it took time and left her open to attacks from the surrounding creatures.

Zhang stayed back as he had before and opened fire with his twin .9mm automatics. He was a very good shot having spent hundreds of hours at a range learning each weapon he owned. He loved the Tommy gun. What it lacked in accuracy it made up for in volume. The Glocks were the opposite. One shot at a time, but they were deadly accurate. He saw what Vampirella was doing and focused on keeping the others off of her.

The plan worked for a few minutes as they cut through two dozen of the undead. The street was lined with dust and empty clothes. But a few had moved past Vampirella and went straight for Zhang. His focus changed and it left her vulnerable. Claws raked at her skin, slicing her open. One of them grabbed her and was going for her neck. She pushed its head back while trying to kick another away. Out of the corner of her eye she saw Zhang firing at the undead going after him and his guns coming up empty.

Jincan tried to move around for another shot on Xuè Lóng. She'd take several and each time her blade just bounced off his stone-like hide. She kept moving, trying to avoid his claws and tail. She knew he wouldn't bite her for fear of her blood. But that was still more than enough to focus on. He took a wild swing with one of his wings and she just dove under it, then had to roll to the side to avoid being smashed by his tail. She found herself directly underneath him and took a swing at his neck. She hoped his underside would be softer. The blade drew a line in the scales, but it was nothing more than a scratch. She rolled back up and started to move, but his claw caught her across the arm. The wound was deep and she could barely hold on to her sword, let alone swing it.

Zhang had one Jiangshi in front of him but saw Vampirella in trouble. Both guns were empty, so he dropped one and dug into his back pocket. He pulled out the two wooden shuriken and flung one into the back of the creature holding her. It disintegrated instantly, freeing her up to defend herself. He jammed the other into the face of the Jiangshi that was trying to bite him. It crumbled away as well. He reached into his bag and pulled out a morning star, then slid it across the ground toward Vampirella.

"Use that!" He pointed to the object a few feet from her.

She did a back handstand and came up with the ancient weapon. It was a giant spiked ball on a wood stick. Something popular in the day of hitting people with metal instead of shooting it at them. The first Jiangshi she hit dissolved instantly.

She looked back at Zhang. "Dipped in her blood too?"

"Of course." He retrieved a couple magazines from the bag.

"You should've given this to me earlier," she yelled, then went back to work killing the undead.

Jincan stood in front of Xuè Lóng, who possessed the body of her brother. To her back was Shanghaied engulfed in flames. Her sword, Soul Eater, rested in her numb hand as blood flowed down her wounded arm. She'd spent six centuries working for this moment.

She spoke through gritted teeth. "Leave my brother's body or I will destroy you."

The dragon's voice rumbled through her bones. "Oh, little squirrel. You still think you have a chance? What is it with heroes and not knowing when they are beaten?"

"You took my brother, my parents, and my life. I am giving you one chance to return to wherever you came from," she said with determination.

"Or what?" He seemed genuinely curious. "Do you really have a plan to stop me? I'd love to hear it. What can you possibly do to me? You can't even raise your sword."

With all of her will, she slowly began to raise her sword. Blood flowed down the blade and dripped onto the ground at her feet. It was obvious that even if she could swing it, she'd have no strength behind the attack and it had done nothing but bounce off his scales when she did have the strength. In a burst of energy, she jerked the sword up and it flew out of her hand.

The sword tumbled as it rose, going just above the dragon's head. He watched it as it went. He seemed so surprised by the move he didn't even try to grab it. He didn't seem to notice the boots running up his back either. Vampirella sprinted up his spine and jumped when she got between his wings. She somersaulted in the air and grabbed Soul Eater by the handle. She twisted her body, bringing the sword around until the point faced Xuè Lóng... then she plunged it deep into his left eye. The blood-soaked blade sliced through the eye and continued into the creature's brain.

Vampirella let go and fell to the ground, landing on her right knee. The Soul Eater began to glow. A bright white light grew out of it, getting more and more intense with every second. She had to cover her eyes. And an instant later the light vanished. She heard the sound of steel bouncing on concrete. She rubbed her eyes to clear them, then finally turned to see.

Xuè Lóng was gone. The body of Fan lay in the street with the sword a few feet away. Jincan walked over to the body and kneeled beside it. Tears streamed down her face. "I have you, brother. It's time to go home."

CHAPTER EIGHTEEN

Zhang moved quickly, bringing his BMW around to load up Fan's body. It was a tight fit, but he got the corpse into the small trunk along with his beloved Tommy gun. Jincan slipped into the back seat while Vampirella climbed up front as he got behind the wheel. He just got moving when emergency vehicles turned the corner. He knew they were too late to save Shanghaied. He had given up almost everything to help save the world. That made him smile.

They stopped a few blocks away at a homeless shelter where Zhang volunteered regularly. He helped sort through the donated clothing. He had to steal a few more items to make his companions less conspicuous. He'd find a way to replace the clothing later. Most of the clothes he grabbed for Vampirella came from the same donor. This time she got a KISS t-shirt and a pair of acid-washed jeans. He found a yellow blouse and a black skirt in Jincan's size.

They stopped at a gas station on the way out of town where the women changed and he topped up the fuel tanks. He also met briefly with a friend who was good at obtaining things. He brought some more ammo, a set of government plates for the car and a few pints of blood. No questions were asked. He poured the blood into a steel commuter cup, grabbed some coffee for himself and Jincan, and they headed out. The trip to Wuhan would take them all night and into the dawn.

There wasn't much talking, but an hour into the trip Vampirella asked, "What was it that brought Xuè Lóng down? Was it the wound? Was it Hua's blood? Was it the enchantment on the sword?"

"I think it was a combination of the three." Jincan touched the sword beside her. "He was incredibly powerful. I think your attack coupled with the toxicity of my blood weakened him enough for the Soul Eater to do its work. I can feel an incredible sense of energy coming from the sword now. More than anything I've ever felt before."

"The spirit of the Blood Dragon is trapped in your sword?" Zhang looked back at her through the rearview mirror. "Is it safe to be carrying it around now?"

"I honestly don't know." She smiled. "But I'm not giving up my sword any more than you wanted to give up your machine gun."

Vampirella looked over her shoulder. "One thing I don't get. Why didn't Fan's body dissolve like all the rest?"

"With the other Jiangshi, we broke the spell that brought them back to life," Jincan explained, "but with Fan, we just pulled the spirit of Xuè Lóng out without disturbing the spell."

They fell back into silence as the car sped north along the G25. Jincan lay down in the back and fell asleep. Vampirella reclined her seat and looked out the window. Zhang didn't know if she nodded off. He didn't know if she even slept. She was different than any other vampire he'd studied, but he hoped to learn more about her in the future. He started running a list in his head of the things he would need to replace now that his home had burned down—his weapons, his equipment—and how much all of that might cost. It was going to take him a long time to put his life back together.

At the next fuel stop, the passengers switched places. Zhang thought about asking one of them to drive for a while, but he didn't know if either one of them knew how. He filled up, got behind the wheel and got them back on the road. The drive continued quietly and they reached their destination about an hour after sunrise. The BMW's navigation system guided him to a plot of land just outside of town. The area was a small park with a section near the back that was fenced in. Jincan got out and unlocked a gate that took them back to the fenced area.

"Is this the farm you grew up on?" he asked.

"Yes." She pointed to a spot next to a stream. "Park over there."

Vampirella sat up in the back. "I thought you lost this after your parents died?"

"I did." She blushed just a little. "But when you live for as long as I have and you deal with the things we do, you get opportunities to use that knowledge to help others. I just happened to help certain people in power who could help me set up this place."

They got out and saw two very old headstones under a tree. She approached them and spoke softly. "I have brought Fan home as I promised."

There was a small shed off to the side, where Zhang found a couple of shovels. He also found two headstones. One had Fan's name along with his birth date and death date. It was the same date as his parents. The other marker had Hua's name on it. It also had that same date of death. He was staring at it when Jincan joined him.

"Jincan may have been on the Earth for hundreds of years, but Hua died that day with her parents." She looked at him sincerely.

"If you are around when I finally go, please see to it that I am laid to rest with my family."

"I will." He scooped up the two shovels and went to start digging.

The fence around the area kept anyone else from seeing what they were doing. With Vampirella's help, it didn't take long to dig a deep enough hole. They found a tarp in the shed and wrapped Fan's body in it before lowering him into the ground. They filled the grave in and put the marker in place. Her brother was finally laid to rest next to her parents. A promise made over six-hundred years before was finally fulfilled. She knelt in front of her family and cried.

They stayed in Wuhan for the day and got a hotel in the city that night. Vampirella felt a bit restless and was ready to move on. She was never a fan of dealing with the fallout of a mission. The cleaning up of bodies, putting back the pieces. Maybe it was wrong of her, but she preferred to deal with the threat at hand then go. She was glad Hua was able to get her brother home, but it no longer involved her. As they drove back towards Hong Kong the next morning, she sat quietly in the passenger seat, contemplating what she should do next.

Without the concern of having a body in the trunk, the trip went quickly and they arrived back at the bar in the early evening. Zhang had wanted to go by and see what was left. They found the street in front cleared and a fence around Shanghaied. He parked the car in the first open spot and they walked the rest of the way.

The fence in front of the building had the name of a construction company hanging on it. The door and the window were completely gone as was the bar and all the tables and chairs. Someone had come in and started cleaning the place out. They could see the damage to the walls and ceiling. All of the mural work was destroyed, but the structure of the building wasn't too bad.

Jincan broke the silence. "Anything that was salvageable was moved to a storage unit. You can come by here tomorrow and the foreman will give you the key."

Zhang looked confused. "Foreman? What foreman?"

She tapped the sign with the name on it. "These guys. I called them while we were in Wuhan. They were told to salvage what they could and clean up the place. They'll be waiting for you tomorrow to go over plans to rebuild. I gave them a budget that will not only get you back in business, but you should be able to upgrade anything you need to."

"What? Uhm... how?" He looked around at the damage. "How can you afford this?"

"Over the years, I found myself with access to knowledge and opportunities that most people wouldn't. During the times I couldn't find Jiangshi to fight, I helped out people with supernatural problems. While I never asked for payment, I took it when one was offered by someone who could afford it. I invested that wisely and with great persistence, I find myself well off."

"What?" The answer didn't seem to make sense to him.

Vampirella leaned in. "She's rich and is paying to replace your bar. Smile and say thank you."

He looked back and forth between the two women then finally nodded his head vigorously. "Yes! Thank you! Thank you!"

She held up her hand to slow him down a bit. "My actions are a bit selfish, I'll admit. I am hoping that you will want to rebuild your lab and armory. I may have finally kept my word to my family, but there are more Jiangshi and other creatures out there, and having your knowledge and abilities would make fighting them a lot easier. Plus, it would be nice to use your guest room when I am in the city."

"Of course." He beamed. "I would be honored to work with you and you can stay here as often as you wish."

"You don't think the Jiangshi are gone?" Vampirella asked. "Xuè Lóng was the source of their power and he's living inside your sword now."

"You said that he had called in only a portion of his army." Jincan leaned back against the fence. "Since he hadn't been on Earth when the army was built up, I have a feeling that they are still around. There may even be more Servants of the Blood out there who could raise more. I won't be able to rest easy until I know for sure."

"What about you?" Zhang looked to Vampirella. "Want to stay and help us chase down hopping vampires?"

"I think Hong Kong is in good hands." Vampirella nodded at Jincan. "I will probably head back to Los Angeles and see what kind of trouble I can get into there."

"Well, you are always welcome here if you come back." Zhang paused for a moment as if remembering something. "If you're not in a rush to get home, I might suggest an interesting stop along the way."

"Where's that?" She was curious.

"You'll see." He started walking down the street. "Come, I'll buy you a donut."

They walked down the street and past the BMW. Two blocks later there was a small shop on the corner and Vampirella could smell the fresh baked goods. The sign was in multiple languages, the English said Ponchik Donuts & Coffee. They walked in and Zhang gestured for them to take a seat at one of the tables. He then went up to the counter and ordered.

"Let me have a half-dozen mixed and three coffees." He smiled to the young lady behind the counter. "And please tell Sergev that Zhang would like to see him when he gets a chance."

She nodded politely, put the order together and then ducked into the back. Zhang carried the coffees and a box of donuts over to the table to sit down. He pointed at a small cake donut with white frosting and chocolate jimmies on top.

"Try the one with the sprinkles," he told Jincan. "It's my favorite."

She picked it up, examined it for a moment then took a bite. It was obvious she'd never had a donut before. Which Vampirella found strange for someone around so long. Jincan seemed to like it a lot, judging by her smile and how quickly she took another bite.

"Sergev makes the donuts," he explained. "He came here ten years ago with his wife. She'd gotten a job with one of the big tech companies and he was bored, so he taught himself to make donuts and opened a shop. During the day you can't even get near the place, it's so crowded."

A large, bald-headed man appeared from the back wearing an apron. He was covered in flour but came out and gave Zhang a big hug. "My friend. It is good to see you. I was so worried when I saw the fire."

"Yes. Horrible thing. But I'm going to rebuild." Zhang slapped him on the shoulder. "It will be better than ever."

"Good to hear." He looked to the ladies. "Who are your friends?"

"This is Ella and Hua." He motioned for Sergev to join them. "Sit, please. I want you to tell them about your recent trip home."

His face changed and he took a step back. "No. They will think I'm crazy. I told you that in confidence."

"They won't think you're crazy." Zhang tried to reassure his friend. "They deal with this kind of thing all the time. I think Ella may be able to help."

He looked unsure, but Vampirella looked him in the eye and said, "It's all right. Please sit and tell me your story."

He took the open seat and leaned in as if not to be heard by anyone else. "I come from the city of Novosibirsk, in Russia. About three weeks ago, I got a desperate call from my sister. Her husband and his friends had gone hunting and did not return. The authorities sent out search parties and claimed to have found nothing. I know the woods back there. She asked me to come look. I headed home immediately and set out to search.

"I knew of a secluded spot he liked to set up his camp, so I started there. What I found was a massacre. There were blood and bones everywhere. Some of them were from the people who had gone in to search for them. I found tracks like nothing I'd ever seen before. I tried to follow them. There was something in the woods. It was big, covered in white fur and moved like a man. But it was no man. I went back to town to get help but was pulled in by the police. They told me that it was a bear that had attacked my brother-in-law. The told me the woods were off limits and they would be dealing with it. They then took me to the airport and sent me back here.

"I have spent many years hunting. I know what bear tracks look like. I can tell a bear from a distance. That was no bear. And I spoke to my sister yesterday. She said more people have gone missing."

The young woman from the counter came around the corner. "Sergev, I need some more glazed."

"Coming." The big man got up. "I'll be right back."

Zhang waited until Sergev had gone before turning to Vampirella. "Well? What do you think?"

She leaned back in her chair and thought about it for a moment. A couple things came to mind that would fit what they were dealing with. Neither of them were good. And all of them were more than normal authorities could handle. She didn't have to be back in Los Angeles immediately.

"Looks like I'm going to Russia."

ABOUT THE AUTHOR

Dan Wickline is the creator of the Legacy of Lucius Fogg novels as well as having written issues of ShadowHawk, 30 Days of Night, Grimm Fairy Tales and his recent hit series The Freeze. He recently teamed with Max Kent on the latest volume of SEAL Team Six: No More, available now, and is working on more new novels for Dynamite Books. If you're a fan of the television series Dexter, you may have seen Dan as comc writer Denny Foster in the second season where he was found dead on a comic shop floor having been killed by a snow globe.

ALSO AVAILABLE FROM
DYNAMITE BOOKS

Shaft - Ernest Tidyman
Shaft's Revenge - David F. Walker
SEAL Team Six Vol 1-6 - Chuck Dixon
SEAL Team Six No More Vol 1-13
SEAL Team Six: AX Vol 1
More Coming Soon!

For more pulse pounding fiction and information on upcoming titles

Visit our website
www.dynamite.com

Like us on Facebook
facebook.com/DynamiteProse

Follow us on Twitter
@DynamiteBooks

And on Instagram
@DynamiteProse

And look for

VAMPIRELLA: BLOOD INVASION

by Nancy A. Collins

available now

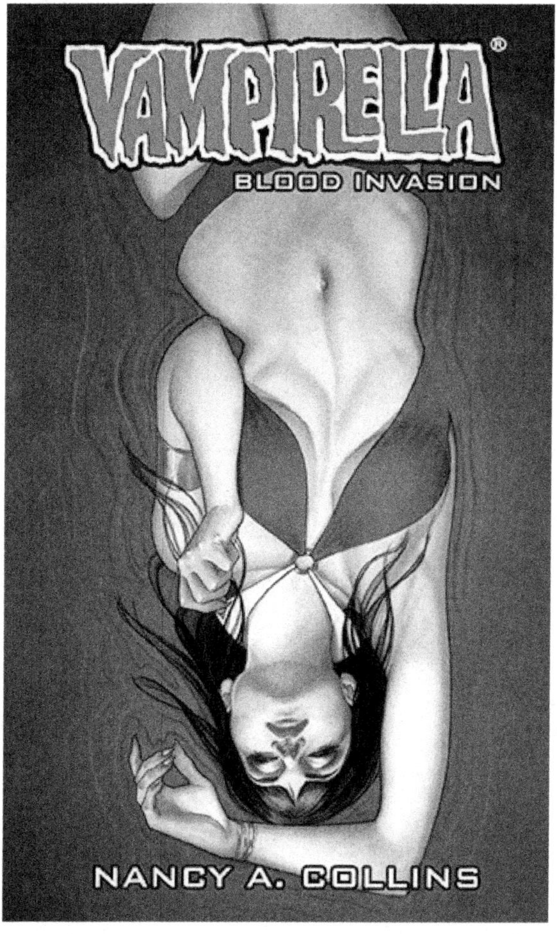

Printed in Dunstable, United Kingdom

79138571R00109